Will   Irma   Taranee   Cornelia   Hay Lin

The Other Truth

Adapted by **ALICE ALFONSI**

HarperCollins *Children's Books*

This book was first published in the USA in 2004 by Volo/Hyperion Books for Children
First published in Great Britain in 2007 by HarperCollins *Children's Books*, a division of
HarperCollins Publishers Ltd.

© 2007 Disney Enterprises, Inc.

ISBN13: 978-0-00-722221-6
ISBN10: 0-00-722221-1

1 3 5 7 9 10 8 6 4 2

The HarperCollins website is:
www.harpercollinschildrensbooks.co.uk

Visit www.clubwitch.co.uk

Printed and bound in Italy

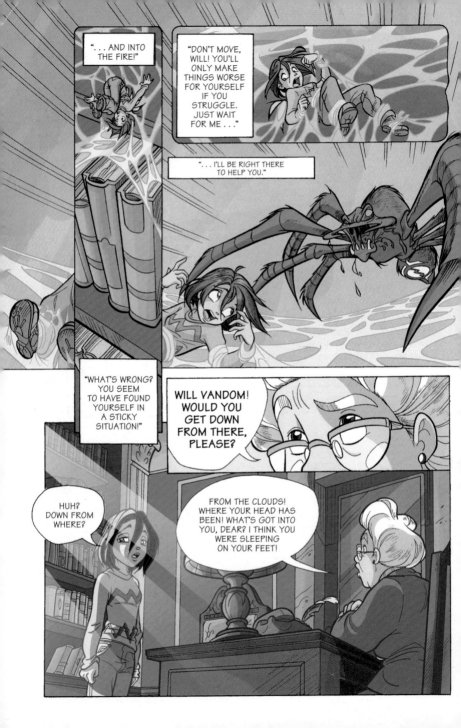

THE ENTIRE TEACHING STAFF HAS NOTICED YOUR DISTRACTION OF LATE. YOU MAY NOT BE ABSENT FROM CLASS, BUT YOU'VE CLEARLY BECOME ABSENTMINDED, MISS VANDOM.

I...I'M SORRY, MRS. KNICKERBOCKER! IT'S JUST THAT...I'VE GOT A BIT OF SLEEP TO...UM...TO CATCH UP ON.

DOES YOUR MOTHER ALLOW YOU TO STAY UP LATE WATCHING TV?

UM, NO. OF COURSE NOT.

THEN DO YOU HAVE SOME KIND OF ROMANTIC PROBLEM? OR IS SOMEONE KEEPING YOU FROM SLEEPING, PERHAPS? A GIRLFRIEND WHO TALKS FOR HOURS ON THE PHONE?

OH, NO! MY FRIENDS HAVE NOTHING TO DO WITH IT.

ARE YOU SURE ABOUT THAT?

?

FROM THE LOOKS ON THEIR FACES, I'D SAY JUST THE OPPOSITE WAS TRUE!

HEY!

YAWN!

HUH?

YOU'RE SO PERKY TODAY, HAY LIN! I GUESS YOU WERE ABLE TO FIND SOME SWEET DREAMS LAST NIGHT, HUH, BRIGHT EYES?

NOT A SINGLE DREAM, ACTUALLY. BUT, CONSIDERING THE ALTERNATIVE, THAT'S TOTALLY FINE WITH ME.

MEANWHILE, TO MAKE UP FOR IT, THIS STRANGE JINGLE HAS BEEN STUCK IN MY HEAD ALL DAY.

THIS IS INCREDIBLE! WE'RE ALL ON THE VERGE OF NERVOUS BREAKDOWNS . . . AND SHE'S WHISTLING!

HEY, WHAT'S GOT INTO WILL?

I DON'T KNOW! SHE'S BEEN ACTING FUNNY FOR A WHILE.

IT'S NERISSA'S FAULT! SHE'S WEARING US ALL OUT! WE HAVE TO DO SOMETHING.

I'VE GOT A SUGGESTION.

LET'S TAKE A NICE LITTLE TRIP OVER TO MOUNT THANOS AND GIVE THAT DREAM-WRECKER A LESSON SHE'LL NEVER FORGET!

ONE

Cornelia rubbed her throbbing head. No sleep and constant worrying about Caleb were really giving her a major headache. And as if that weren't bad enough, she had to listen to her best friends arguing.

For what seemed like forever, the five Guardians had been under assault. Nerissa was entering their dreams and turning them into nightmares. Now that school was over for the day, the girls were trying to figure out how to defend themselves against the evil woman. But nobody could agree on a course of action.

Sitting beneath the swaying oaks of Sheffield Institute, Cornelia crossed her legs. Fallen leaves rustled against her long fuchsia skirt, and light gusts of wind

1

sent more foliage fluttering down. The random bits of colour swirled around before drifting lazily towards the manicured grass.

When she was little, Cornelia had thought of the autumn leaves as tiny colourful kites. Every year she had chased them as they fell, and pasted her favourites into a scrapbook. Now that she was older, they seemed more like jagged teardrops, symbols of nothing more than the end of summer, the end of green, the end of warmth.

A shiver ran through her. As she rubbed her arms, a bright golden leaf landed lightly on her head. She abruptly brushed it away.

I've got to think about Nerissa now, she told herself, not these fall leaves.

Since that vengeful being had emerged from her volcanic tomb, she'd grown extremely powerful and dangerous. Cornelia knew that the Guardians would have to be very careful and very smart in the way they fought Nerissa.

What we need is a *real* plan, thought Cornelia, a clever strategy. Maybe if Nerissa has a weakness of some kind, an Achilles' heel, we could use it against her.

How were the Guardians going to discover

that weakness? Cornelia had no idea. But there was one thing she did know. Irma's suggestion that they "take a nice little trip over to Mount Thanos" was totally nuts.

Sitting beside Cornelia on the grass, Hay Lin responded to Irma's gung ho – and incredibly crazy – proposition by furrowing her brow. "You want us to go and fight Nerissa *on her own turf*?" she asked.

"Of course!" Irma replied. "What have we got to be afraid of? Together we can beat her!"

Cornelia sighed. It was *so* typical of the water girl to jump in headfirst without asking how deep the pool was. Then again, thought Cornelia, just letting anything pour out of her mouth was pretty typical of Irma, too.

Hay Lin's dark, almond-shaped eyes widened in apprehension. "I don't think the Oracle would agree with your plan," she said to Irma.

The Oracle was the powerful, all-seeing being who watched over all the worlds. Or, as Irma might put it – he was their cosmic boss.

The whole Guardian thing had started with Hay Lin's grandmother, Yan Lin, who had once been a Guardian herself. She had revealled to

Will, Irma, Taranee, Cornelia, and Hay Lin (whose initials formed W.I.T.C.H.) that they weren't just average girls. Each of them had a special power. Taranee's was over fire, Irma's was over water, Cornelia's was over the earth, and Hay Lin's was over the air. The fifth power, over energy, belonged to Will, the Keeper of the Heart of Candracar, the miraculous crystal that united the other four girls and magnified their abilities.

The five friends had been chosen to become the next generation of Guardians. Using their powers, it was up to them to protect the earth and the other worlds from evil and to guard the portals that linked the worlds.

From the start, the girls had been in awe of the ethereal, immortal Oracle, the being who'd entrusted them with their mission. But after what he'd just done to them, the Guardians were beginning to wonder if they could ever trust the Oracle again.

"The Oracle?" Irma flapped her hand in a dismissive wave towards Hay Lin. "Don't you remember how he treated us the last time we saw him? To avoid a battle with the old hag, he made us forget about her completely."

"And about Caleb," Cornelia said, her head suddenly feeling too heavy to hold up. Closing her eyes, she pictured him – Caleb, her sweet, wonderful, brave rebel. As her chin sank down, tears welled up beneath her eyelids. One slipped through and drifted down her cheek. "I love him, but even so I forgot about him."

"It was the Oracle's magic," Hay Lin quickly reminded her. "You couldn't help it!"

Cornelia shook her head. She still couldn't believe that with a simple spell, the Oracle had erased her most precious memories. "I guess that's true, but then I wonder . . . is magic stronger than love?" She opened her eyes and found the other Guardians staring blankly at her.

They don't understand what I am feeling, Cornelia realised. It was one of the reasons that she missed Caleb so badly. He understood her like no one else – her feelings, her mind, her heart. And she understood his.

That's what love is, thought Cornelia. So how could some stupid magic spell have made me forget him – even temporarily? Is it my fault? Is my love for Caleb not strong enough?

She sighed, unable to stop beating herself

up. On the other hand, she thought, maybe the magic had worked because Caleb himself had been created by magic. . . .

Prince Phobos, the evil and unlawful ruler of Meridian, had transformed him from a flower in his garden. At first, Caleb had been changed into a Murmurer, one of the brightly coloured beings Phobos used in order to spy on his own subjects. But Caleb had refused to remain in Phobos's service. Once he saw the injustices being done to the Meridian people, he had decided to fight the evil prince.

With the strength of his spirit and will, Caleb had evolved. He broke away from the spell that bound him and changed his destiny. He became human – and, oh, what a human! Cornelia sighed at the memory of his sparkling eyes, blue as a mountain lake, his strong body, soft brown hair, and iron jaw, as firm as his steadfast spirit.

Before Cornelia had even visited Meridian, she'd dreamed about Caleb. On the day she'd finally met him, he'd saved her from drowning in a watery portal. Then he'd helped save his own world by leading the Meridians in their rebellion against Phobos. But now his life was hanging by a thread. The reason? Nerissa. And the Oracle.

Cornelia grimaced. If the Oracle hadn't wiped my memory clean, I would have gone to Caleb sooner!

Caleb had been captured by Nerissa's servant Shagon, who had taken him to her lair on Mount Thanos. Cornelia and the Guardians would have stopped at nothing to save him. The Oracle knew that, so he'd wiped out the Guardians' memories to keep them from confronting Nerissa at the place where she was most powerful.

Cornelia still didn't understand why the Oracle had done that. Wasn't he supposed to be *protecting* other beings? Wasn't he a force for good? How could he have been so cruel? So heartless?

By the time Cornelia and the rest of W.I.T.C.H. had regained their memories and raced off to help Caleb, he was barely alive, a frozen rag doll in the ice and snow of Nerissa's volcanic mountain. Nerissa hadn't killed him, but she'd battered his soul. She'd drained everything from him. Sure, W.I.T.C.H. had rescued the former rebel leader from Nerissa's final blow, but Cornelia feared her one true love still might not survive.

The Guardians had brought Caleb to the only place that could restore him – the lofty world of Candracar. This was where the Oracle lived. It was Caleb's home now, too, because Caleb was serving the Oracle as the Herald of Candracar.

When Caleb first pledged his service to the Oracle, Cornelia had accepted their separation as a long-distance relationship. She was happy because she knew that Caleb was out of danger. He was alive and well. And he had assured her that one day they *would* be together. But, at the moment, Cornelia wasn't so sure.

Nerissa had really damaged Caleb, and only the Oracle had the power to save him. So Cornelia had to trust him. When the Oracle had commanded the Guardians to leave Candracar and go back to their earthly lives, they'd had no choice.

Once again, Cornelia was forced to abandon her one true love – and ever since, she'd been torturing herself about that spell. How could it have made her forget Caleb?

As Cornelia sat on the chilly Sheffield

Institute lawn, gazing into her friends' concerned but clueless faces, a part of her felt even more alone. How could she explain what she was going through to her friends?

When you love someone and he loves you, his well-being is everything to you, thought Cornelia. If he suffers, you suffer. And when you feel as though you've let him down, it's . . . *devastating*.

Hay Lin, Irma, Taranee, and Will were pretending to understand, but Cornelia knew they really didn't. They'd never really been in *true* love. Not the kind of love that she and Caleb shared.

"In any case," said Hay Lin, breaking into Cornelia's thoughts, "we can't judge the Oracle's decisions."

"Says who?" barked Irma, giving Hay Lin a look. "Where is it written?"

Hay Lin frowned at Irma. A dark expression crossed her pale features – as if she were about to tell Irma to knock it off. But Hay Lin never got the words out. Taranee leaped to her feet first, shouting, "All right, all right!"

The girls instantly quieted down, then stared at their freaked-out friend. It wasn't like

Taranee to get so worked up. Usually, she was calm and reserved. But now, behind her big, round glasses, Taranee's brown eyes burned with righteous anger.

"The problem right now isn't the Oracle!" she cried. "It's that woman! Don't you guys see what she's doing to us?" Taranee clenched her fist and shook it. "She's filling us with doubt. She wants to weaken us. To bring us to the breaking point!"

Cornelia found herself wondering . . . Could Nerissa be the reason I'm so upset about the memory spell? Could her influence be making me doubt myself even more?

Yes, Cornelia realised, it could very well be possible. "You know, Taranee," she said, lifting her head and brushing some strands of blonde hair away from her eyes, "I think you're right."

That's when Will finally spoke. "She's snooping around in our dreams, frantically sifting through our thoughts. But she only wants one thing. . . ."

Will lifted her head. She focused her gaze on her hand. A few moments later, the very thing that Nerissa so desperately wanted appeared in the palm of Will's hand – the

Heart of Candracar, the one source of all the Guardians' strength.

"Well, let her come and get the Heart!" Will cried, rising to her feet and holding it before her. "I'm ready for her!"

The other Guardians gawked at their leader, whose voice suddenly shook with an awesome fury. It was a bit of a shock, since Will's voice had been pretty weak in school that day. And ever since they'd come outside she'd been acting dazed and sort of out of it.

But she's not out of it any more, thought Cornelia. For a moment, Will's energy channeled itself through the Heart. The perfect crystal transmuted its Keeper's fury into a brilliant pulse that flared bright as a celestial star.

Cornelia raised her arm to shield her eyes from the dazzling flash. *Wow*, I can't believe how much Will's changed. And not just in the last hour.

Cornelia still remembered the day she'd met Will Vandom, the new girl at Sheffield – a short redhead with a shy personality and tomboy clothes. Cornelia hadn't seen one shred of leadership ability in the nervous, self-conscious girl. Will herself had expressed doubt about the prospect of being the Keeper of the Heart.

Cornelia, on the other hand, had been the confident Infielder at school, super popular, with tons of admirers. She'd been the bossy one, the organiser. So at first, she had been confused, annoyed, and a little bit jealous of Will's being handed the Guardian leader role.

But her feelings towards Will had changed . . . quickly. Under pressure, Will's shakiness evaporated. In her role as the Guardian leader, she'd displayed courage, cunning, and confidence. Cornelia, on the other hand, had to admit to herself that she'd let herself become consumed, and sometimes even crippled, by her worries about Caleb.

I can actually *feel* the waves of strength emanating from Will, Cornelia realised. There's no way I could muster that kind of energy. Not while I'm so wrecked over Caleb.

With Nerissa out to destroy the Guardians and steal the Heart, Cornelia knew that Will would be under more pressure than ever. Her position as leader had never been harder, and Cornelia didn't envy her.

As the afternoon sun sank lower, the Guardians finally broke up their meeting and headed home. Cornelia walked through the Sheffield gate, and another stray leaf fluttered down, landing on her head. This time, however, she didn't brush it away. Instead, she found herself taking it in her hand and twirling it in her fingers.

She had to admit, the fiery colours really were impressive – red, yellow, orange, and the faintest trace of green still running through its veins. It reminded Cornelia of the Guardians' Aurameres, the five colourful orbs that each held one of the Guardians' unique powers.

It's so strange, she thought, how, in just a few short months, a simple leaf can mature and change so much – from a tiny bud to a flat green palm to this amazing display of blazing colour.

"Maybe this one's worth hanging on to," she whispered to herself. Then she pocketed the leaf and strode away.

TWO

The Oracle, small and serene, knelt on a floating platform of shimmering gold. Before him an enormous crystal revolved in midair. Upon its surface the Oracle observed a reflection of the Guardians in Heatherfield.

Beside the Oracle stood his faithful adviser, Tibor. Dressed in a flowing robe, the old, wrinkled man stroked his long, white beard. His snowy hair was even longer than the beard. And his bushy eyebrows were as thick and white as the clouds that surrounded the Temple of Candracar.

"Interesting," said the Oracle, observing the Guardians. "What the other Guardians see in Will is only one aspect. But there are more than one to consider. Like this meditation crystal." The Oracle gestured to the large, gleaming crystal revolving in front of him. "It is cut to display many facets. If you observe only one, you will never see the whole gem. The whole truth."

"You are speaking of the Keeper of the Heart?" Tibor asked the Oracle. "Do you think the Guardians are misunderstanding her?"

"Yes. Partly." The Oracle nodded his bald head, which was as smooth as Tibor's face was wrinkled. "What the Guardians saw in Will was defiance and fury," he told Tibor. "Her friends assumed she was reacting to Nerissa's threat. She was. But there is another, more serious concern in the Guardian leader's mind. That concern is what prompted her furious outburst."

Tibor nodded. He lifted his old eyes and pointed to the magical image of the red-haired Guardian. "I sense a deep sadness in her, Oracle."

The Oracle sighed. "It is the heaviness of the Heart, Tibor. The Heart of Candracar."

The conflict within Will was nothing new to the Oracle. He had witnessed such internal struggles many times. The worlds over which the Oracle watched were like vast, blue pools. Each one swirled and churned with millions of different waves – millions of different beings struggling with one another and with themselves.

One small stone could cause a ripple in any one of those pools. The ripple might at first appear minor, but the Oracle knew it could build in strength and effect. It could change a wave's direction and destiny. It could push a being one way or another, towards the darkness or the light.

This was not an easy thing for a young mind to grasp, and Will was struggling with it now. What had happened to Nerissa could happen to any being . . . even to Will herself. The Oracle had seen it many times from his airy perch. He'd watched evil take shape and injustice reign. His efforts to protect the good were not always successful. Not even in Candracar . . . and that was what pained him the most.

"The Guardians are in danger," Tibor reminded the Oracle. "What will happen next?"

"I can't answer you!" replied the Oracle with uncharacteristic shortness.

Tibor's bushy white eyebrows rose. The

Oracle saw at once that he'd alarmed his adviser, but this situation was very difficult for him. He closed his eyes and tried to reclaim his tranquillity.

"I am not infallible," he reminded Tibor. "Nerissa is living proof of that."

The Oracle's voice was much calmer than it had been before, but a single crease remained in his otherwise smooth brow. He had been so pleased a generation ago – during Yan Lin's generation – when he had anointed Nerissa the fifth Guardian and the Keeper of the Heart.

At that time, the Oracle had seen in Nerissa only goodness and strength, courage and light. She was like the smooth, calm surface of a pool. The Oracle could not then foresee the ripples that would one day flow through her, the storms that would form in her spirit. Nor could he foresee the terrible choices she would one day make. He could only watch and react when she finally made them.

There was nothing he could do to change Nerissa's will. Good and bad were present in every being, magical or ordinary, mortal or immortal – one had to choose for oneself.

The Oracle's gaze shifted from Tibor back to

the swirling images in the large, revolving meditation crystal. He listened to more of the Guardians' thoughts and feelings and raised an eyebrow.

"Will is not the only one to suffer," he told Tibor. "Cornelia is doubting her own love."

"Look," said Tibor, raising a knobby finger. "Something is coming from the Guardian's mind."

The Oracle watched Cornelia release a sentiment so powerful it materialised and floated all the way up to Candracar. The Oracle stretched out his hand and caught the pure, white feather of thought.

"It's about Caleb," he told Tibor. A slight smile blossomed on his lips as his heart lightened. "Let us bring it to him. It will do him good."

Tibor nodded and followed the Oracle as he made his way through the vast Temple of Candracar. There was nothing like this place – not on the earth or in any other world. The rooms they moved through were miles high. The walls were of iridescent crystal, intricately carved with elaborate designs and symbols. The floors were encrusted with dazzling gemstones. There were sapphires, emeralds, rubies, and strange glowing jewels from worlds on which no human being had ever walked.

The air was so pure it filled the Temple with a sweet, intoxicating scent. The air made the etched crystal walls sparkle with a brilliance almost unbearable to the human eye. Beyond the vast, glassless windows were no mountains or trees, no roads or buildings – simply an infinite sky of blue and lazily drifting clouds.

There were places in the Temple for all sorts of purposes – for meditating, for meeting, for judging, for conjuring, and for healing. The Oracle and Tibor were on their way to a healing place, where Caleb had been taken after the Guardians had rescued him from Nerissa.

"Unfortunately," said the Oracle as he moved through the Temple's endless halls, "Caleb's young life weakens with every passing moment."

Tibor nodded sadly. "I see and sense that, as well, Oracle. . . . But I often wonder how all of this could have happened."

The Oracle fought a flicker of frustration. "The Altermere," he replied, struggling to remain serene. "Everything started with that."

"Yes," said Tibor.

The Oracle was still saddened by the way the Altermere had come into being. Luba, a member of the Congregation, had from the beginning disagreed with the Oracle's decision to entrust the young Guardians with the power and responsibility of protecting the worlds. She had thought the girls immature and careless. So she'd watched and waited in the Temple for a chance to sabotage them.

It had been Luba's duty to protect the Guardians' Aurameres – the colourful glowing orbs that held the girls' powers. But because of Luba's disagreement with the Oracle and her desire to prove herself right, she had failed in that duty. Instead, she'd entered Aura Hall and cast a spell to bind four of the orbs together. The huge explosion that followed had rocked the Temple. And on the earth, four of the Guardians had suddenly lost their powers.

When the explosion was over, the Aurameres had formed an Altermere, a mindless blue blob that held the four Guardians' powers within its form. Instinctively, it went to the earth, to be united with the fifth.

"When the Altermere arrived at Cornelia's

door in the shape of one of her Guardian friends," the Oracle explained to Tibor, "she embraced it, and the five powers were finally united in one Guardian – Cornelia. She chose to release all five powers into Caleb."

Caleb needed those powers. After the battle to save Meridian, Prince Phobos had been so angry with Caleb for fighting against him that he'd returned the boy to his original form – a flower. Cornelia had saved Caleb. The five powers she'd placed in him had turned him from his flower form back into a Murmurer. And it was finally her loving teardrop on his hand that had made him human again. Even after he'd become human, however, a copy of the five powers still remained inside him.

"That is why Nerissa captured him," the Oracle continued. "She wanted the Guardian powers that Cornelia had given him."

"Then Nerissa holds a copy of all five powers?" Tibor shuddered at the thought.

The Oracle nodded. "Yes. She drained the powers from Caleb while she held him on Mount Thanos. Unfortunately, she drained almost everything else from Caleb, as well, including his spark of vital energy."

The Oracle and Tibor had finally come to a great archway. It framed a vast room in the Temple, in which an entire wall was missing. In its place was a vertical whirlpool of dazzling, crackling energies.

"We have arrived," he told Tibor. "This is the entrance to the Cosmos of Abeyance."

The Oracle gazed through the tall portal of swirling light. Shimmering rays flowed from its edges, bathing the room in a glowing silver-blue. Caleb was somewhere deep inside. The Oracle could just feel the boy's limp form and semiconscious mind.

The Oracle glanced back at Tibor. "I sense that you have not stopped asking questions."

Tibor scratched his beard. He was clearly having trouble perceiving any sign of Caleb inside the swirling Cosmos. "Um . . . actually," he said, "I would like to hear the sound of *answers*."

The Oracle sighed. "Believe me when I tell you that not even I know what lies beyond this threshold. The Cosmos is a place of healing. It lies at the boundary between existence and oblivion."

Tibor remained silent. The Oracle could feel

the old man's apprehension. This was not a place any being would wish to find itself. In the Cosmos, Caleb lacked memory, he was devoid of identity, he was without pain or pleasure.

The Oracle knew that the blonde Guardian blamed him for this. He'd observed Cornelia earlier calling him cruel and heartless for temporarily wiping her memories clear of Caleb. She had accused the Oracle of failing to protect the boy's life.

The Oracle sighed. Cornelia's vision was simply too narrowly focused, he thought. He'd often observed humans making this mistake. They would stand too close to a subject and only see one side of it, as if they were standing before his meditation crystal and peering into only one facet. Cornelia was not standing back far enough to see the whole truth.

Protection had been the Oracle's primary concern all along. He'd been protecting the Guardians from themselves. And he'd been protecting Caleb, too. If he had allowed the Guardians to go after Caleb immediately, Nerissa would have destroyed them *and* Caleb on Mount Thanos. The Oracle's spell had allowed time to pass. Enough time for Luba to come to terms with her transgressions.

When the Guardians finally did arrive to rescue Caleb, Luba was there, ready to help them. She had been the deciding factor in that battle. Luba had held Nerissa at bay so that the Guardians could take Caleb and escape.

In the process, Nerissa had burned Luba badly. For the rest of her immortal life, Luba would be forced to wear the painful scar bearing Nerissa's mark. But Luba's sacrifice meant that the Oracle could forgive her and release her spirit from any further punishment. Luba was free.

Without the Oracle's spell, the Guardians, Caleb, and Luba would have been lost. With the spell, the Guardians were saved. Luba was redeemed. And Caleb had a fighting chance. . . . Still, the Oracle was saddened by the brave boy's present state . . . so lost . . . so weak.

"Hope that you will never find yourself here, Tibor, as our young Herald has," the Oracle continued. Then he opened his hand and released Cornelia's pure, white feather of thought. The feather floated in the clean air of Candracar, then passed through the crackling energies of the cosmic whirlpool.

"Thanks to this feather," said the Oracle, "the landscape of the Cosmos will transform around Caleb, and it will let him relive moments of his past. It will sift through the ruins of his memory and allow him to redis-cover small remnants of life . . . minuscule yet indispensable granules of existence. . . ."

The Oracle closed his eyes. With his aware-ness, he followed the feather as it fluttered and swirled, then finally spiraled down on to Caleb's forehead.

Instantly, the boy's blue eyes opened. "Where am I?" he rasped.

The delicate purity of Cornelia's memories touched Caleb's mind, awakening his past. Within the Cosmos, Caleb saw stone buildings and narrow streets, creatures of different colours and sizes.

"What is this place?" he whispered. And then he knew. "Of course! It's Meridian. My city! How could I have not recognised it?"

The Oracle observed Caleb as the boy's memories came back to him. He took in a scene of children playing in the street in the unique, coppery light of his world's afternoon sun.

"Yes," he murmured. "It's my city. The colours, the smells, the sounds . . . but also the suffering . . ."

The sky abruptly darkened. Caleb saw Prince Phobos's big, ugly guards taking prisoners, setting fires, and terrorising innocent men, women, and children.

"I see it now. . . ." Caleb whispered. "I remember . . . the pride of people battered and oppressed by an unjust tyrant. The dream of a better life, the hope to one day see the return of the light of Meridian . . . the return of Elyon."

The Oracle knew that now Caleb remembered it all: how he'd been transformed to a Murmurer; how he'd spied on the people for Phobos. He knew that now Caleb remembered the guilt and anger he'd felt after seeing the results of his spying. Entire families had been thrown into the prince's dungeon. Innocent people had been starved and brutalised. Caleb was remembering the moment he became a rebel.

Suspended within the whirlpool, Caleb's hands balled up in angry fists. He remembered the path he'd chosen. How he'd made the decision to change his destiny, to fight Phobos . . .

and he remembered Elyon, Meridian's rightful heir . . . the golden-haired girl he'd helped to place on the throne. . . .

Outside the swirling Cosmos of Abeyance, the Oracle nodded. He was pleased with Caleb's progress. The sweet memories of Cornelia had revived the boy and begun to restore him. . . .

Standing beside the Oracle, Tibor spoke, his voice hopeful. "I feel something, Oracle. Something is awakening. But what?"

"Identity, Tibor," the Oracle whispered with a hopeful smile. "Minuscule yet indispensable granules of existence."

THREE

"You really want to know what's bothering me?" asked Will.

Hay Lin swiveled her desk chair around and shot Will a look that said, *You're kidding, right?*

Will shifted on Hay Lin's bed and bit her bottom lip. She knew what Hay Lin was thinking. It seemed really obvious what was bugging her – Nerissa. That's probably why Hay Lin invited me back here, thought Will. She probably wants to make sure I'm handling the pressure OK.

When they'd first arrived at the Silver Dragon, Hay Lin had insisted they share a pot of herbal tea and a plate of almond biscuits. To Will, it almost felt like old times, with Hay Lin's

28

grandmother sitting right there next to them. But the old woman had passed away. These days, she resided in Candracar with the Oracle. And in Heatherfield, the Guardians had only one another to confide in.

After Will drained her teacup, the girls headed upstairs to her family's cosy apartment. Now Will sat in Hay Lin's bedroom, trying to make her understand the thing about Nerissa that was *really* bothering her.

OK, Will thought, this isn't going to be easy. All the Guardians think they know what's making me freak out, but the truth isn't so simple. "It's the fact that the Heart of Candracar once belonged to Nerissa," Will confessed to Hay Lin.

Hay Lin tossed one of her black pigtails over her shoulder. She pulled off the green-and-yellow goggles she liked to wear as a funky headband and tossed them next to her computer. "Will, um . . . how do I put this? Duh!"

"No, no, no." Will shook her head again. "You still don't get it."

Hay Lin furrowed her brow. "What's not to get? When my grandmother was a Guardian, Nerissa was the Keeper of the Heart. Now

Nerissa wants to steal it back and destroy us. We all heard the story."

Will chewed her thumbnail. What Hay Lin said was true. The Guardians had gone to Candracar to get some answers. And Hay Lin's grandmother had provided them . . . even though it had been in the weirdest way possible.

She'd taken them to her "crypt of memories" – a fantastic, domed room in the Temple of Candracar. Golden vessels with jeweled stoppers held the old woman's many reminiscences. Floating blue bubbles protected the vessels, providing the magic that fed her memories and kept them alive.

The memory of Nerissa came out of one of those vessels. It had been a tarnished one. Since she'd arrived in Candracar, Yan Lin had never opened it. She'd buried it far below the other golden vessels, but when the Guardians asked for answers, Hay Lin's grandmother willingly dug it out.

She opened the vessel and shuddered, calling its contents the most unpleasant memory of her life – and Candracar's darkest hour. Nerissa had been Yan Lin's best friend and a fellow

Guardian. She had been the Keeper of the Heart. But one day Nerissa had turned on the other Guardians. Will could still hear the shakiness in Yan Lin's voice as she recalled what had happened to Nerissa. . . .

"She was consumed by the Heart's infinite power, and wanted it solely for herself!" Yan Lin had told the girls.

Nerissa had betrayed her friends and defied the Oracle. And what had led to her downfall? *Her obsession with the Heart.* That was what had scared Will the most.

"Hay Lin, listen to me," said Will. "If Nerissa was chosen to be a Guardian, it means that in the beginning she was a good person . . . and that she became evil later on."

"So what?" cried Hay Lin, throwing up her hands. "You aren't anything like her!"

Will frowned. Sure, she wasn't anything like her *now*, thought Will. But wasn't that the point?

"Don't tell me you're afraid of going nuts and ending up like her," Hay Lin said. "Come on, that's crazy!"

Will didn't think it was so crazy. She moved slowly to the window and stared out at the steel-and-glass towers of Heatherfield. The sidewalks were much less crowded at that hour, and the bumper-to-bumper traffic had thinned to the *whoosh, whoosh* of a few passing cars.

As she watched the streetlights flicker on, Will quietly sighed over the timing of all of it . . . just when the other parts of her life were getting on track. She and her mother were finally – and amazingly – on good terms. She was doing well in her new school. She and Matt were actually beginning to understand each other. And she was at last feeling that she'd proved herself worthy of being the leader of the Guardians.

But Nerissa's nightmares and her dark influence were shredding Will's peace of mind. Falling asleep in class was only part of it. The strain was making Will impatient with her mother, as was the feeling that she was blowing her chances with Matt.

Even worse, she couldn't stop obsessing about what had changed Nerissa. Had the power of the Heart itself somehow warped her? Had the pressure of being the Keeper sent her off the deep end?

Will caught a reflection of her face in the

darkening window glass. Her brown eyes were red-rimmed from lack of sleep, her hair looked like a tangle of red snakes, and her skin was pale as a ghost's.

Whoa, not good, thought Will. If Matt sees me like this, he may never ask me out again.

Will turned to face Hay Lin. "What if being Keeper of the Heart is a sort of curse?"

Hay Lin sighed. "What if you just need some sleep?"

Will actually smiled at Hay Lin. Funny how Hay Lin is the one taking charge and giving advice, she thought. I'm usually the one to do that – but then Hay Lin *is* Yan Lin's grandaughter. Great wisdom seems to run in the family.

"Then again," Hay Lin continued, "since you're asking so many questions, maybe you're actually expecting some answers?"

Answers? Will thought. What's she talking about?

Hay Lin moved to her desk and opened a shoe box. Inside was a stack of envelopes. She reached in and pulled one out.

"What's that?" asked Will, a little nervous. Could Hay Lin have actually found the answers she'd been looking for?

"It's a letter," said Hay Lin. She opened the envelope and withdrew a folded piece of paper, which she held out to Will. "That's really why I asked you to come here."

Will took the folded paper. The paper was brittle and slightly yellowed with age. She gingerly opened it.

"It belonged to my grandmother," Hay Lin explained. "I found it in her things."

"What does it say?" asked Will, trying to skim the small, delicate handwriting.

Hay Lin shook her head. "What it says isn't as important as how it was signed. Look at the initial."

Will's eyes skipped down to the signature. "It's a *K*," she whispered. She tried to guess whose it could be. Her mind ran through the names of the other Guardians with whom Yan Lin had served. There was Nerissa . . . Duh! . . . and Cassidy, Halinor, and . . .

"*Kadma!*" cried Will. "The old Guardian!"

Hay Lin excitedly nodded her head. "It must be. I don't remember her knowing anyone else with the initial *K*."

"OK," said Will, "so where is Kadma now?"

Hay Lin tapped her chin. "Well, we know

what happened to Nerissa . . . and Cassidy."

Will shuddered, wishing she could forget that part of Nerissa's story.

"And we know what happened to my grandmother," continued Hay Lin.

Will nodded. Yan Lin had been taken to Candracar after her death, and honored as a Guardian.

"If there were two other Guardians in Candracar, she would have told us," said Hay Lin.

"And we know Kadma and Halinor haven't responded to roll call," Will pointed out.

"That's why I'm convinced the other two are here – on earth," said Hay Lin.

Will agreed. "That's what I think, too."

"Look. It'll be easy to track down the person who sent this letter." Hay Lin pointed to a seal on a corner of the envelope. "It's the logo of an association based in – "

Will leaned closer to read the address, and her jaw dropped. "Fadden Hills?" She couldn't believe it. Yet there it was, in embossed gold letters: FADDEN HILLS.

Will's mind went back in time. She sighed as she remembered her old hometown and the people she'd known when she'd lived there.

I wonder if the town's changed much in the past year? she asked herself.

She guessed it probably hadn't.

Fadden Hills wasn't the kind of place that saw a lot of changes. It was a lot smaller than Heatherfield and further north. So it was probably a lot colder there now. There were no skyscrapers, smog, or crowded sidewalks. Traffic jams were pretty much nonexistent.

Will remembered the town's main shopping area, lined with old-fashioned lampposts. There'd been all sorts of cute little shops up and down that cobblestoned street. She recalled how much she'd enjoyed wandering in and out of them. She remembered the ice cream parlor, the amazingly delicious hot-fudge sundaes. In the summers, she used to get them with extra whipped cream, then hang out with her friends on the town green.

Funny, she thought, it all seems so incredibly long ago now, like another lifetime.

Faces raced through her mind – teachers at her school, her old babysitter, a favourite neighbour, her first swim coach. She hadn't kept in touch with any of them since moving to

Heatherfield, not even the girls her own age who had been her friends.

Now Hay Lin is telling me that Kadma is hiding out in my old hometown, thought Will. But why?

She sighed in frustration. She had wanted this letter to give her the solution to their problems – but it only presented more questions. Now she and Hay Lin would have to go to Fadden Hills and ask them.

Will couldn't imagine what sort of answers they were going to find in her old hometown. But a weird sensation in the pit of her stomach made her wonder if she was ready to hear them.

FOUR

Mount Thanos was not what it initially seemed to be. On the outside, glacial winds chilled a barren landscape and gave the appearance of calm. On the inside, it was a different story. Molten lava seethed and churned.

Nerissa was just the same. For centuries she'd been entombed in this volcanic mountain, but time had not cooled her blistering fury or warmed her coldhearted calculations. For her crimes, Nerissa had been tried, sentenced, and punished by the Oracle and the Congregation of Candracar, but she had never repented. On the contrary, she felt even more justified than before for the terrible things she'd done, the lives she'd taken.

Over the many long years, the icy sea's lapping rhythms had sustained Nerissa's chanting incantations of hate. The scorching heat of the bubbling lava had stoked her vows for revenge.

Standing before her now were three prime examples of her spiteful stamina – her servants, Ember, Tridart, and Shagon.

Conjured from the elements around her, Ember and Tridart were Nerissa's unique creations, extensions of her own dark magic.

Ember, a winged female, had skin of black ash and hair of red flames. She had been fashioned from the volcanic lava boiling in the pit of Nerissa's mountainous lair. Heat and fire were her weapons.

Tridart was Ember's exact opposite. White as the snow layered on Mount Thanos's frozen rocks, his bald head was as smooth as ice, and his crystalline armor harder than diamond. Nerissa's magic had carved him from the coldest, most ancient glaciers on the planet.

Despite the care with which she'd fashioned these two, however, Nerissa was less than thrilled with their achievements. Even worse, they had begun to bother her with irritating and mindless questions, making their already dull companionship even more tiresome.

When the two finished uttering their final question, Nerissa reared back and raged at the pair. "It is not your job to think!"

Ember and Tridart cowered before their mistress, bowing their heads. As they backed away, both glanced worriedly behind them.

Stupid, stupid, servants! Nerissa silently railed. Don't they know they are nothing more than expendable extensions of my will? How dare they pose questions to me!

"But, Nerissa . . ." said Shagon, stepping forward to defend his fellow servants. "Ember and Tridart only asked you – "

Nerissa held up her hand. "Silence!" The word echoed off the craggy walls of the vast rock cavern.

Her blue eyes, once hollow pits, turned colder than the frigid sky above her lair. "I know what my devoted little creatures asked me!" she told Shagon. "Why don't I attack the Guardians? Why don't I take back the Heart of Candracar? The point is, I didn't create them to make small talk. They don't think. They act. Nothing more!"

With a sigh of disgust, Nerissa began to

pace, using her tall staff as a walking stick.

Even when I directed Ember and Tridart to act, they failed me, she thought. I sent them to hold the Guardians at bay and kidnap Caleb. And they botched both jobs. If it hadn't been for Shagon's intervention, Caleb might have slipped through my fingers. . . . Then again, Shagon is the strongest of my creations.

As the incarnation of Nerissa's own hate, Shagon had trumped the little blonde earth girl. When Cornelia saw Shagon grab her beloved, she'd released a torrent of emotional rage. Shagon had fed on it. The girl's hate had made Shagon strong enough to break free of the Guardians and whisk Caleb back to Mount Thanos.

Once Nerissa had drained the five powers from Caleb, everything had changed for her.

The centuries of entombment had ravaged her physical form, giving her the appearance of an ancient crone. Her hair had been filthy straw, her teeth rotten and broken, her form thin and bony, her skin dry as brittle parchment, and her eyes cold and empty.

Absorbing the five Guardian's powers had regenerated her exotic beauty. Her dark hair was now long and lustrous, her skin creamy and smooth, her eyes a brilliant blue, and her lips plump and pink. She now appeared as young, perfect, and powerful as she had long ago, when she'd been a Guardian, the Keeper of the Heart. Even her scarlet gown appeared new again, the fabric's silk and velvet clinging to her newly voluptuous shape as it luxuriously brushed against her skin.

Nerissa narrowed her glowing blue eyes on Shagon. She was pleased to have the brawny monger in thrall. But she didn't care for his defense of the fire-and-ice couple.

"You, Shagon," she said. "When it comes to my creations, you are quite different. Isn't that right?"

"I am your faithful servant, just like the others," he said.

But Nerissa knew that that wasn't true. She hadn't created Shagon from lifeless elements as she had her other servants. Before she'd transformed him, he'd been a man. She'd plucked the visiting geologist from Mount Thanos's volcanic rim and engulfed him with her powerful magic. Now his thick blonde mane of hair framed a face pale and blank – a face like a puppet's, strung out on Nerissa's dark spell. Still, Nerissa knew that deep inside Shagon's mask were the brains and will of a living, flesh-and-blood man. She couldn't take any chances. She had to discourage him from thinking or acting for himself.

Nerissa faced Shagon. "Tell me," she purred, "was it you who put those questions in the minds of your little friends?"

"And if it was?" asked Shagon.

Nerissa smiled, amused by her human puppet. "You're a sly one, Shaggy," she had to admit. "I should punish you for your insolence, but if I did, I would do so with *hate*."

It was how she'd created him in the first place, by channeling her own centuries-old rage.

"You thrive on that beloved feeling, don't you?" said Nerissa. "Which is why it will be your dear companions who'll do the punishing for me."

With a snap of Nerissa's fingers, Ember and Tridart moved in to torture Shagon. And Nerissa moved out through the mouth of a nearby tunnel.

"Aaaargh!"

Hearing Shagon's screams of pain behind her, Nerissa shook her head and muttered, "How tiring it is to manage the servants."

For centuries, of course, Nerissa had not been troubled by such things as managing servants. She'd been entombed inside this otherwise uninhabited piece of rock, surrounded by a vast ocean. Even after all these years, she was still stung by the Oracle's words before the Congregation of Candracar. "Confined within the depths of Mount Thanos, deprived of her powers, with neither aid nor companionship," the Oracle had decreed. "That is our decision!"

Of course, Nerissa had vowed revenge. "I will return," she'd shouted at the Oracle and his minions, "and you will regret having stood in my way!"

She'd been sealed up in a tomb of stone with seemingly no chance of escape. For centuries, she'd listened to the ebb and flow of the frosty tide, the molten ooze of the red-hot lava. For centuries, she'd seethed, hating and cursing those who had trapped her, vowing to destroy them all if she ever got the chance.

Her release seemed impossible. Nerissa's only chance at being set free was in the highly unlikely event that the five Guardians' powers were reunited. Thanks to Luba, the Keeper of the Aurameres, the impossible had come to pass.

As Nerissa moved through one of Mount Thanos's shadowy rock tunnels, she cackled to herself. If only she could have seen the Oracle at the moment when he realised one of his own Elders had been responsible for reuniting the five powers: Luba, a member of his own Congregation of Candracar! The irony was too great.

Nerissa sighed in disgust. The Oracle was so vague, so weak. He lacked the will to put a swift, violent end to his enemies.

Even me, she thought. Not only couldn't he bring himself to destroy me, he couldn't even pronounce a limitless sentence! The fool! His naive belief in good led him to provide me with the tiniest ray of hope for my release. Perhaps he thought I might one day repent, change, and see the light of day again.

Well, it happened, thought Nerissa as she walked towards the faint glow at the end of the tunnel. The five powers came together and cracked my tomb like an egg, giving me new life. The impossible became possible. But I'm not about to repent or change. If anything, I'm even more determined to assert my dark powers, more determined to destroy those who imprisoned me and reclaim what they stole from me: the Heart of Candracar.

Nerissa closed her eyes. The very thought of the Heart made her swoon. When she was its Keeper, it had been everything to her. Like a beating organ, it had been a part of her body, mind, and spirit. Its pulsing light had sustained her, fed every fiber of her being. When the Oracle took it from her, pronouncing her unfit to be its Keeper, she had lost her mind. In order to get it back, she had killed Cassidy, the Guardian to whom the Oracle had entrusted it.

"I killed once to get the Heart," she hissed. "And I will again."

Nerissa opened her eyes. Suddenly exhausted, she leaned for a moment against the mouth of the rock tunnel. Her head was pounding now, and she was having a little trouble breathing.

The mere task of carrying the five powers was in itself an incredible strain. And without the Heart of Candracar, Nerissa was severely limited in what she could accomplish.

But *with* all five powers *and* the Heart inside me, she thought, imagine what I could do! A shiver of excitement raced through her at the thought.

No one had dared unite the Heart and all five powers in a single being. It had been more than forbidden. It had been *unthinkable*. But Nerissa was certain of one thing. Whoever did it would be wielding the most awesome power the universe had ever seen!

"I will have the power to destroy them all," Nerissa murmured to herself. "The Oracle, the Elders, and all of Candracar! That is why I must put a final end to those young, ridiculous Guardians and take back the Heart that is rightfully mine!"

Unfortunately, Nerissa knew, that was easier said than done. Which was exactly what she would have told Ember and Tridart if she had bothered to answer their questions.

"The truth is," she murmured, "I can't attack the Guardians directly. I have to limit myself to exploring their dreams. I have to drain them, weaken them, before I act."

Nerissa moved out of the dark tunnel and

stepped into a cosy space much smaller than the vast main cavern she'd left behind. Beautiful aqua bunting was draped over the rock walls. A thick rug covered the floor. And gilt-trimmed furniture filled the space. In the corner, beside Nerissa's bed, sat a small stone gargoyle. It looked like an orange creature with pointy ears, a long tail, and batlike wings. In its claws it held a primitive flute.

Snap!

With the flick of her fingers, the gargoyle came to life and began to play its instrument. A trilling melody filled the makeshift little boudoir. It was a strange and eerie tune – and, to Nerissa, a familiar one. As it played, she made her way over to the bed.

"The problem is these journeys into the world of nightmares," she murmured, sinking into the green velvet bedcovers. "They're exhausting me."

For many weeks now, Nerissa had been using her dark magic to spy on the Guardians. In the shooting flames of Mount Thanos's volcano, she had visions of them. Through elaborate spells, she had entered their dreams.

The whole scheme had started with Will. At

the time, the young Keeper had been on vacation at the beach with her Guardian friends. She had fallen asleep on a towel, beneath the warm sun.

Nerissa had invaded Will's pleasant dream of swimming, whispering a series of disturbing comments to her.

There is a great weight bearing down on you . . . something that oppresses you . . . and I know what it is. . . . It's the Heart of Candracar!

In her dream, Will began to fall through the water. She became confused, not knowing which way was up. She began to feel panic. She thrashed and kicked, frantic to find a way back to the surface. But as she began to climb, a pair of gnarled hands reached for her legs and pulled her back down.

Give it to me, and set yourself free from the suffering! Nerissa had demanded in Will's watery nightmare.

Down, down, down Will was pulled. But the determined girl would not give up the Heart. In her sleep, Will had cried out her protests. She had awakened on the beach within a circle of concerned friends.

After that day, Nerissa had visited Will's

dreams many more times. And each time, she'd twisted Will's dream into a nightmare.

She'd made Will fall from a great height. She'd terrified her with giant snakes. She'd set her home on fire. She'd shrunk her down to the size of a fly and forced her to face a giant spider.

Time after time, Will had remained strong. She had refused to give up the Heart. And Nerissa had found her annoying little friends to be just as challenging!

Nerissa had visited each of the Guardians in turn – Irma, Cornelia, Taranee, and Hay Lin. just as she had with Will, she had entered their dreams and transformed them into terrifying nightmares, too.

But not one one of the Guardians would agree to turn on Will and make the Keeper give up her Heart!

Nerissa's patience was wearing thin. But she was not discouraged. Not yet.

She vowed to continue her fight. She would prey on the girls' doubts, weaknesses, and worries. She would heighten their fears and suspicions. She smiled at the thought of wearing those scared little girls down.

One day soon, I will have have what I want, she thought. The Heart of Candracar. The power to exact my revenge!

As the sound of the magical flute flowed over her, the familiar melody danced and trilled, taking the former Guardian back to a time of her own youth – a time of great energy, strength, and confidence.

Trilee, trilee, trilee, lee, lee . . . Triloo, triloo, trilooooo!

The melody soothed her pounding head and frayed nerves, and Nerissa's eyelids were soon feeling heavier and heavier.

Before sleep finally claimed her, Nerissa's mind reached out. With her dark powers, she conjured up a dream to spy on the little Guardians.

I wonder what the Heart and its Keeper are up to, she thought before drifting off. Or should I say, the Keeper of *my* Heart?

FIVE

Hay Lin laughed as she rode the crackling energy currents. With glee she twirled on its supersonic gusts – until familiar, flutelike notes hit her, with the force of a hammer!

Trilee, trilee, trilee, lee, lee . . . Triloo, triloo, trilooooo!

The next thing Hay Lin knew, her body was slamming into something tall and solid. *Wham!*

"Oh, no!" Will rushed over to her. "Hay Lin! What happened? Are you OK?"

Sprawled on the snowy sidewalk, Hay Lin closed her eyes and put a hand to her aching head. "That . . . that music . . . I'm hearing that music again!"

"You really got hit hard," said Will, helping Hay Lin to her feet.

No, thought Hay Lin, Will doesn't understand. It was the other way around. The music hit me *first*; then I struck the post.

"Oooooh, I remember now," she said, brushing snow off her jacket. "We're in Fadden Hills, right?" She looked around. The walls of her bedroom were gone. So were the skyscrapers of Heatherfield. Gone, too, was the balmy fall weather of their seaside city. Fadden Hills was farther north – *much* farther north. The town's streets and sidewalks were already blanketed with the first snow of the season, and the temperature was close to freezing!

Hay Lin and Will hadn't wasted any time getting there. After Will had read the letter from Kadma, they'd thrown on their jackets and concentrated. Will had touched her index fingers together, and she and Hay Lin had both focused their minds on Fadden Hills.

The next thing Hay Lin knew, her limbs were turning invisible, just as they had the first time she'd transported. Hay Lin had been minding her own business in a Green Bay bus station when, without any warning, one of her hands had vanished, then another, and, finally, her whole body.

After she'd turned invisible, a force had whisked her high into the air, pulling her like a magnet towards her destination. She'd reappeared with Irma in Riddlescott Lake, where Will and Cornelia had been trying to save Caleb from Nerissa's servants. Will, with the help of the Heart, had transported Hay Lin and Irma from the bus station to the lake.

Hay Lin thought that this time seemed a lot like that first time. Her physical body had turned transparent before takeoff, and then she'd whooshed high into the sky on a rush of crackling energy. She and Will had risen above the skyscrapers of Heatherfield, then travelled north over the countryside to Fadden Hills.

The first time Hay Lin had transported, she hadn't known what was happening or where she would end up. So the whole trip had been a little frightening. But this time, she knew exactly what was happening to her, and she'd really enjoyed herself – until the *end* of the trip. She'd just been slowing down, preparing to land, when that trilling melody had entered her head.

Too weird, thought Hay Lin. That same tune had been warbling around inside her head since she'd got up that morning. But she didn't know why. She hadn't heard it on the radio or anything like that. Actually, she'd never heard the melody before in her life.

Even stranger, music usually conjured up some sort of meaningful sensation for Hay Lin. It spoke to her through memory or feeling. But this tune evoked absolutely nothing in her. The piece was totally without spirit. The notes felt empty.

Hay Lin sighed. I guess it's just a harmless little jingle, she thought. But the way it keeps haunting me is really starting to creep me out!

"How's your head?" asked Will, looking concerned. "Do you remember what we were doing?"

Hay Lin nodded. "To get here, we decided to use our powers. Yeah, we transported ourselves."

"The problem is that you knocked into that post." Will pointed to the tall, old-fashioned lamppost on the Fadden Hills sidewalk. "Why didn't you see it?"

Hay Lin considered telling Will she'd been assaulted by a piece of music, but that sounded completely mental, so she kept it to herself. The most likely explanation was that she just wasn't used to transporting and she'd probably messed up the landing herself. After all, thought Hay Lin, this is a brand-new power, and it's never easy to master a new Guardian ability!

"I don't know exactly what happened," Hay Lin told Will. "One thing's for sure. I must have hit the thing straight on. I've got a splitting headache. . . ."

"I'm really sorry, but we have to move quickly," Will said. Then she sighed, admitting, "The Oracle doesn't want us to use our powers for personal reasons, but . . ."

"This is an important trip, just like a real mission. I know," said Hay Lin.

They'd already discussed it back in Hay Lin's bedroom. And they'd firmly agreed that they had no choice – nor did they have the time – to travel to Fadden Hills the old-fashioned way. A bus ride would have taken too much time, and neither one of them could have afforded a plane ticket.

Will glanced around and shook her head. "I grew up in this town, and I don't believe in coincidences. Kadma's letter came right from here. I have to find out why. To understand."

"OK," said Hay Lin, "but why didn't you want to tell the others anything?"

Will sighed. "I didn't feel like listening to Taranee's advice, Irma's wisecracks, and Cornelia's . . . *comments.* . . . I have the feeling this is something really personal."

Hay Lin saw Will's eyes become distant and glazed over as she took in the streets and buildings of her hometown. Fadden Hills was a lot smaller than Heatherfield. It was almost quaint, with lampposts instead of streetlights and cute, old-fashioned shops on its main street, with nothing like Heatherfield's modern skyscrapers, bumper-to-bumper traffic, and edgy city kids . . . just a few cars and pedestrians and a group of giggling girls making a huge snowman in the middle of the town square.

As Hay Lin walked along next to Will, the snow crunched under her shoes. Will snapped the hood of her jacket over her shaggy red hair and wrapped her arms around her slender torso. Hay Lin didn't have a hood. Her pigtails swirled in the cold wind as she shoved her hands into the pockets of her short grey jacket.

We aren't dressed for this weather, she

thought with a shiver. For sure, my leg warmers and skirt weren't the warmest choices. We should be wearing boots like every other pedestrian on this sidewalk.

The men, women, and children they passed were all bundled for the weather in wool caps, gloves, and scarves.

They certainly were used to an early snow around here, thought Hay Lin. Which meant that Will had been, too – when she lived there. It was weird for Hay Lin to think about her friend's having lived a whole entire life before they'd met. Hay Lin wondered what it had been like for Will there. Did she miss it?

Hay Lin also wondered how Will felt about coming back. The town must have held a lot of memories. Hay Lin thought that Will was probably remembering some rough times. On the other hand, Will could have been remembering the good times.

Hay Lin considered asking Will about all that but decided they had enough to think about already. If Will talks, I'll listen, she thought. Otherwise, it's probably better for us both to just focus on finding Kadma.

Since Hay Lin didn't know the town, she

relied on Will to lead the way down its main street. The little shops were really adorable – a bakery, an antiques store, a tea shop. There was a really cute arts and crafts store with glass beads and silk flowers in the window. If they hadn't been on a Guardian mission, Hay Lin could have easily spent hours there.

They passed a café, a women's clothing boutique, and a hardware store. At the end of the street, Will suddenly stopped.

"What's up?" asked Hay Lin.

Will pointed. Hay Lin saw that they were standing in front of an ice cream parlor.

"Ice cream? You're kidding, right?" said Hay Lin. "I'm freezing my buns off as it is."

"Best hot-fudge sundaes I ever had," Will said a little wistfully.

"Do you miss them?" Hay Lin asked.

Will shrugged and turned away.

Hay Lin caught up to her and touched her arm. "Will, its OK. Let's go back," she said. "You haven't been back here in a long time. You can stop in and get one if you want. . . . I mean, at least it's *hot* fudge on the freezing cold ice cream, right?"

Will didn't respond. She just kept walking.

They turned a corner, then another. Eventually, they came to an area of the town where there were tall, old trees and very wide sidewalks. The houses were large and set far back from the road.

"*Cypress Hills,*" Hay Lin read aloud from a small street sign. She turned to Will. "Ever been to this neighbourhood?"

"No." Will shook her head. "All I know is that it's a really ritzy residential area."

The girls continued down the long, scenic street. It was completely deserted. No cars were even parked on the road, since each sprawling home had big driveways with four- and five-car garages. As the afternoon shadows lengthened, the only sound they heard for many minutes was the crunch of their shoes along the ice-encrusted snow.

As their steps fell into a rhythm, Hay Lin couldn't stop that strange, trilling melody from playing again through her head. . . .

Trilee, trilee, trilee, lee, lee . . . Triloo, triloo, trilooooo!

Over and over it played. . . .

Trilee, trilee, trilee, lee, lee . . . Triloo, triloo, trilooooo!

"We found it!" Will suddenly cried. "This is the address."

Hay Lin followed Will up to an elaborate, wrought-iron gate. Flanking the gate were tall stone pillars, overgrown with vines. One of the pillars displayed an aqua-coloured plaque. A star had been engraved on the plaque above the words RISING STAR FOUNDATION.

This has to be the place, thought Hay Lin. That star logo is the very same one embossed on the corner of Kadma's envelope.

Stepping up to the closed gate, Hay Lin pushed it. "Locked," she told Will. She peered through the filigreed swirls in the wrought iron. On the other side, a long path led to a mansion with marble columns and a grand, arched door-way. Around the large building were acres of land.

"The grounds look like a nature preserve," said Hay Lin.

How cool is that? she thought. This should be really interesting!

She glanced over at Will, who appeared to be looking for a way in. "Well?" said Hay Lin. "What are you waiting for? Ring the bell!"

Will had found something on one of the

stone pillars. It looked like a speaker box – the kind someone inside would use to talk to someone standing on the outside. She wrestled with the overgrown vines, obviously looking for a button or doorbell near the box to alert the people inside.

"I *would* ring the bell," she told Hay Lin in a frustrated voice, "if one would just appear out of nowhere!"

Suddenly a creaky voice spoke through the crackling intercom. *"Crrr . . . follow . . . crrr . . . cheepee . . ."*

Will turned to Hay Lin. "Did you get what that voice told us?" she asked. "Who are we supposed to follow?"

Hay Lin nervously chewed her thumbnail. "A certain 'cheep' or something?"

Cheep!

The girls looked up to see a large blackbird staring down at them from the top of the stone pillar. Its dark feathers gleamed as it sang out a few notes of a tune.

Trilee, trilee, trilee, lee, lee . . . !

Weird, thought Hay Lin. Is it just me, or is that bird's song just like the tune that's been in my head all day? But before she could ask Will about it, someone inside hit a buzzer that released the lock.

Bzzzz! Ker-chunk!

The big iron gate swung open.

The blackbird cheeped again and flew down. The girls watched it settle on the long snow-covered path. Will shrugged and followed the blackbird. Curious, excited, and a little bit freaked, Hay Lin followed, too.

Call me a scaredy-cat, she whispered to herself, but I've got to wonder what we're getting ourselves into!

SIX

What are we getting ourselves into? Will asked herself.

The blackbird flew straight as an arrow towards the enormous mansion, as if it had done so a thousand times before. Then it veered off. Turning a corner, it led the girls to the side of the building.

If you ask me, thought Will, "Cheepee" up there is downright creepy.

When the bird fluttered through a small open panel in a towering set of double doors, Will paused and waited for Hay Lin to catch up. Her heart pounded as she cautiously pushed open one of the tall, heavy doors.

Given the weird way they'd entered the

place, with vines overgrown on the front inter-com and the strange bird as their guide, Will half expected to enter a haunted house. But instead, she and Hay Lin stepped into an enor-mous, glass-enclosed greenhouse. Attached to one wing of the mansion, the place was jammed with colourful flowering plants, lush green shrubs, and exotic fruit trees.

Hay Lin's jaw dropped. "Take a look at this place!"

Will nodded, eyes wide. "This is amazing!"

The faceted glass in the walls and ceilings magnified the weak winter sunlight, making the room warm, bright, and cheerful. It reminded Will of the way the Heart magnified the natural abilities of all the Guardians.

It's a room of endless summer, thought Will. And the snow piled up outside just makes it seem all the more magical.

Cheep!

Will looked up to find that their feathered friend had landed on the branch of a large plant. Next to the plant was a cosy little gather-ing of three wicker chairs. In the centre of the circle of chairs was a low coffee table on top of which sat an ornate silver serving tray holding a pitcher of water and three glasses.

Hay Lin walked over to the furniture and plopped down on one of the chairs. "A black-bird for a butler and a greenhouse for a waiting room," she said as she closed her eyes. Will saw her friend's nostrils flare as she inhaled the scents of lavender, mint, oranges, and flower petals.

Will was too nervous to sit down. First she craned her neck to check out the tall, curved, glass ceiling; then she began to walk the floor, her mind racing. Coming back to Fadden Hills had dredged up all kinds of memories. Some were good, some bad, and some in-between. So many different feelings were tangling together inside her right now that she could barely sort them all out.

On the one hand, it was cool to see the old streets and shops, to hear girls giggling as they built a snowman in the town square. Will remembered doing that with her friends back when she had lived there. She had good mem-ories of being on the swim team at school and going to basketball games on Friday nights. But the very best – and worst – memories for Will were the memories of her home life.

As Will paced uneasily inside the green-house, observing the various plants and flowers, she continued to sort through all the good and bad memories. Suddenly, she stopped. Near an elegant arrangement of potted palms, dozens of framed photographic portraits of children and teenagers were on display. A large sign hung near the photos. She pointed to the sign and called back to Hay Lin.

"Read this!" Will cried. *"The Rising Star Foundation helps children with neither homes nor families – "*

From across the room, a woman's gentle voice interrupted. "Many of these children are now successful businesspeople. They are now well integrated into society."

Will turned to find a woman walking towards them. She had dark brown, almond-shaped eyes, and over one shoulder hung a single long black braid, heavily threaded with grey. Her eyebrows were grey, too, but her skin was still flawless and smooth, with only the faintest wrinkles at the edges of her eyes and mouth. She wore a lovely gown of purple velvet with long sleeves and a high neck. A sky-blue shawl was draped gracefully over her arms, and she held a leather-bound book.

Wow, thought Will, watching the woman glide across the greenhouse floor. This must be Kadma. She's so elegant, poised, and dignified. Will couldn't help comparing the appearance of this former Guardian to her own frantic reflection in Hay Lin's windowpane, less than an hour before – a giant mess of red tangles, with bloodshot eyes.

I wonder if I'll *ever* be as together as Kadma, Will found herself thinking. Years from now, will Matt ever see me as elegant and dignified? Will tried not to laugh out loud at that idea. Long shot, she decided. *Definitely* a long shot!

"You!" By now, the older woman had reached the circle of wicker chairs. She was looking at Hay Lin as if she'd just recognised an old friend and couldn't quite believe her eyes. "You must be Yan Lin's granddaughter! May Candracar rest her soul."

"And you must be Kadma, right?" Hay Lin guessed.

The woman's gaze shifted. "And this is the one and only Will." Her tone seemed strained, almost wary. "She always said that you'd come here."

Will was taken aback. I never met this woman before, she thought. So how does she know me?

"She . . . *who?*" Will asked Kadma defensively. "How do you know who we are?"

"I know many things," said Kadma. She crooked her finger and Will approached and followed her as she walked over to the collection of framed portraits near the Rising Star Foundation sign. As they came nearer, the children's faces grew older, into the faces of teens and young adults. Kadma pointed to a cluster of them. "Look carefully at these pictures," she told Will. "Do you recognise anyone?"

Will gaped at the familiar faces in the photos. "But I . . . I don't understand!" she cried.

Hay Lin heard the alarm in Will's voice. "Will," she said urgently, "who are those people?"

Will pointed to a young woman in a college graduation cap and gown. The woman had long, light brown hair and wore wire-rimmed glasses. "That's Miss Pibbleton!" Will cried. "She used to be one of my teachers."

When Will had known the woman, she'd been older and had worn her hair shorter. But the wire-rimmed glasses were exactly the same.

Will's gaze frantically moved from photo to photo, face to face. "There's – there's another teacher . . . and even my first swimming coach! And . . . and . . ."

This can't be happening, Will thought, feeling her pulse race. I'm going to lose it! This can't be real!

She started to bite her nails. She was so freaked out she actually felt dizzy. But it *was* real, and she knew it.

"There were many others," Kadma informed her. "All young people whom our association helped at one time. They were people who watched your progress and helped you when you were in need."

Coming back here had been hard enough; all the memories – good and bad – weren't something Will really wanted to deal with. But *this* . . . Will had never expected to hear this!

"And then, they would report everything to Halinor," Kadma continued to explain. She gestured to the photo of a lovely blond woman in a blue business suit with pearls around her neck.

Halinor? Will repeated to herself. She

remembered the name. Halinor was another of the five Guardians who had served with Kadma, and Hay Lin's grandmother, and Nerissa.

"You were her protégé," Kadma informed Will.

That's news to me! Will thought. It all seems so unreal. These people . . . all these people whom I knew and trusted, who were supposed be taking care of me, watching over me; they were *spying* on me the whole time I knew them. They were reporting my every move to a woman I'd never even met!

Will's spirit sank like a stone. She felt like such a fool . . . so completely betrayed. All these people . . . they'd all been wearing masks! They'd been . . . lying to her!

Who am I supposed to trust now? she wondered, shaking her head. My mother's wrapped up in dating my history teacher . . . even the Oracle seems to be turning a blind eye to the threat of Nerissa. . . .

Kadma slowly wandered back to the wicker chairs and sat down near Hay Lin, who, for her part, looked totally confused. "I created the Rising Star Foundation with Halinor," she continued, utterly oblivious to Will's turmoil. "But now I'm alone."

Hay Lin cleared her throat. She appeared to be waiting for Will to say something, but Will seemed dumbfounded, still staring up at the gallery of faces from her school, her neighbourhood, her family's circle of friends. Her whole life here in Fadden Hills had been under a microscope, and she hadn't even known it.

Finally, Hay Lin asked Kadma the question that Will would have asked if she hadn't been so overwhelmed. "You're saying that you were *spying* on Will . . . the entire time she lived here, before she moved to Heatherfield?"

Kadma looked away from Hay Lin, completely ignoring her accusatory question.

"Will," she called sharply, "take this!"

Will turned and walked slowly over to Kadma. The former Guardian held out the leather-bound book she'd been holding since she'd entered the greenhouse.

"Halinor wanted me to give it to you," she told Will.

Will took the book from the older woman's slender, manicured fingers.

"It's the only reason I allowed you to come

inside," Kadma confessed to them. Her voice was cold again, brittle as the icicles hanging outside her perpetually summerlike waiting room.

The room was suddenly too hot, and the revelations upsetting. Will felt herself perspiring. She ran her hands over the leather-bound book, flipped it open, and saw what it was. "A diary? . . . I don't understand."

Will glanced up expectantly into Kadma's dark eyes, but the woman simply looked away. "My bird will show you the way out," she snapped. "Goodbye!"

What? Will couldn't believe it. Kadma was giving them the brush-off. She was already rising from her wicker chair and gliding out of the room.

Will chased after her. "But . . . but you can't do this!" Her voice was pleading, desperate. Kadma refused to turn around. That was when Will became downright angry. "You can't rip my life apart and just walk away!" she shouted.

Kadma wheeled abruptly. "I owe you nothing! Nothing! Understand, little girl?" Her voice was so sharp and fierce that Will took a step back.

Hay Lin quickly jumped up from where

she'd been sitting and raced over to help Will.

"Once I was a Guardian," Kadma continued to rage. "But now I'll have nothing to do with you! So leave! Get out! Now!"

As Will stood staring, frozen in shock, Hay Lin put an arm around her shoulders. She glared at Kadma. "Don't you yell at my friend!" she cried. Then she called up to the blackbird butler. "Come on, bird! Get us out of here before things get even worse. We know when we're not welcome!"

Cheep! Cheep! the bird cried as it lifted off its perch and flew in circles over the girls.

"Yeah, little fellow!" called Hay Lin, leading Will away. "I know it's not your fault." To show her friendship for the bird, Hay Lin began to whistle: *"Trilee, trilee, trilee, lee, lee . . . Triloo, triloo, trilooooo!"*

"That melody!" cried Kadma. She went completely pale. Putting a hand to her head, she began to sway. "It can't be. . . . It can't . . ."

Kadma's angry expression had crumbled into one of shock, then pain. Her proud shoulders slumped, and she suddenly looked old and fragile. Then her eyelids fluttered and she began to fall.

Oh, my gosh! Will thought.

Hay Lin was right behind Will as the two girls rushed to catch Kadma before she hit the ground. Will took one of her arms, Hay Lin the other, and they carefully helped her over to a wicker chair.

"Hay Lin, what did you do to her?" Will whispered.

Hay Lin's eyes widened. "Who? Me?" She was just as surprised as Will to see Kadma's reaction. This visit was certainly not what Hay Lin had expected. Nor, for that matter, was Kadma. Hay Lin wondered what other secrets the old Guardian held and whether she would share them with the girls.

SEVEN

As she collapsed into the chair, Kadma raised a shaking hand to her throbbing head. She asked for a glass of water, and Will poured one from the pitcher on the coffee table.

"Here," Will said softly, holding the glass out to her.

Kadma nodded her thanks. Her hand continued to shake as she took the glass and brought it to her dry mouth.

That melody, she thought, *that cursed melody! It's brought all the wretched memories back!*

For years, Kadma had lived her life trying to forget. *Why had these girls had to come here?* she silently lamented. *Why had they invaded her privacy? Poisoned her* perpetual summer garden with chilling memories?

Yan Lin's granddaughter stepped forward, trying to explain. "I was just whistling that song that's been running through my mind for days . . ."

Kadma's breath caught as she realised the terrible truth. If that song was in Hay Lin's head, then there was only one possible reason. "Nerissa has returned," she whispered with deep regret. "If I'd known that before . . ."

". . . You wouldn't have acted like a grouchy old woman?" Will finished the sentence for her.

Kadma waved her hand. These girls, she thought. They're so young. They just don't understand what it is to age, to lose your abilities, your place in the cosmic scheme.

"That's just how I am," she told them. "Once I held the power of earth!"

"Earth," Hay Lin repeated. Then she winked at Will. "I get the connection. Our Cornelia is quite the *easygoing* type herself. . . ."

Kadma could tell that Hay Lin was kidding around. But there was nothing about this situation that was in the least bit funny – not to her. "That melody you were whistling was composed by a former Guardian," she informed Hay Lin.

"Nerissa?" Hay Lin asked in surprise.

Kadma nodded. "As a girl, she was a musician," she informed them. "She jokingly called that little tune 'Nerissa's Trill.'"

In her memory, Kadma could still see Nerissa's fingers flying up and down the keys of her exquisite silver flute. Back then, Nerissa's tune had been a joy to hear. But everything back then had been bright and new and green, thought Kadma, full of budding promise.

Yan Lin, Halinor, Cassidy, Nerissa, and I, she thought. We were all so happy, so proud to be Guardians! To be entrusted by the Oracle of Candracar with amazing powers and responsibilities! But the best part of all was that we were the best of friends.

Kadma could hardly fathom all that had happened to them over the years. She lifted her head to meet Hay Lin's eyes. "In those days, Nerissa and your grandmother had a very close friendship."

"Maybe that's why Hay Lin is immune to Nerissa's nightmares," Will speculated.

"Perhaps," said Kadma. "In any case, we

can take that song as a warning. It's the sign that Nerissa is alive and seeking revenge."

Will stepped closer, her expression earnest. "Since our mission began, we've been looking for answers."

Answers? thought Kadma. She sighed and thought, These girls have not yet learned. The questions that they want to ask do not have simple answers.

"Why did you try to make us leave before?" asked Will.

"Simple," Kadma replied. "You represent a past that I'm trying to forget." She met Will's eyes. "Once I was as you are now, proud of being a Guardian. But then . . ."

Again, Kadma put a hand to her aching head. That cursed melody was still echoing in her ears, piercing her heart, her mind, her spirit. "When Yan Lin told you our story, she didn't tell you the whole truth."

Will exchanged a worried look with Hay Lin. "Tell us," she whispered.

Kadma nodded. "There was a moment when the Oracle understood that Nerissa could no longer be the Keeper of the Heart of Candracar."

Kadma still remembered that day. . . . Nerissa had once been a force for good. But she'd changed over the years and slowly begun to use the Heart for her own selfish ends. She'd bullied and overpowered innocent people to improve her position or flatter her vanity. And she had not used the Heart for its intended purpose – to battle evil – but just to keep herself safe.

The Oracle knew all that, of course. He'd been watching Nerissa all along. But he'd also been waiting.

"After observing Nerissa, the Oracle decided that the only one capable of keeping the magic crystal was Cassidy," Kadma informed Will and Hay Lin. "He took the Heart from Nerissa, and he entrusted it to her."

Kadma squeezed her eyes shut and took a deep breath before conveying the next part of her old memory. "Blinded by jealousy, Nerissa lured Cassidy into a trap and did away with her." That terrible moment had haunted Kadma all of her life.

"After Nerissa was banished, Halinor and I found ourselves before the Elders of Candracar," Kadma told Will and Hay Lin, "and we accused the Oracle. He had seen Nerissa's obsession and known what might happen to Cassidy, but he gave her the Heart all the same!"

Tears welled up in Kadma's eyes as she ended her story. . . . "That's why you'll never see Halinor or me joining the Elders in Candracar. Because we questioned the Oracle's authority."

Will looked stunned by Kadma's tale.

Hay Lin stared in disbelief. "So you'll never have a place in the Congregation? You were an *outcast*?"

Kadma could hear the incredulity in the little Guardian's voice. Yan Lin's granddaughter did not want to accept the truth about the Oracle – how harsh he could be. But it is *true*, thought Kadma. Halinor and she *were* outcasts.

"I don't understand," said Hay Lin, her voice now clearly distressed. "What about my grandmother?"

Kadma quickly turned to the girl and put a hand on her shoulder. "She didn't agree with us, but we remained friends."

Then Kadma turned to address Will, but she found the girl completely shocked. The young Keeper of the Heart stood with her eyes wide and her jaw slack, clutching Halinor's leather-bound diary to her chest.

"So it's true," Will said, her voice barely above a whisper. "The Keeper of the Heart is cursed."

Kadma turned from Will to Hay Lin and back to Will. These girls had been brave to come there, she realised, and clever to track her down. Now that she knew that they would be forced to fight the evil Nerissa, Kadma's heart went out to them.

I've been so lost in my own self-pity, she told herself, that I've forgotten what it's like to carry such heavy responsibility at such a young age. These girls don't need my sad stories; they need my support.

That's right, Kadma! She could practically hear Halinor's voice scolding her. *Enough with feeling sorry for yourself! It's time for you to make me and Cassidy proud – you owe us that much!*

From the depths of her heart and soul, Kadma agreed. She turned to Will. "No! The Keeper of the Heart is not cursed," she assured the young Guardian. "It's a privilege to be the Keeper, and it is your destiny." Then, in a warm, encouraging voice, she added, "You were born under a lucky star . . . the star of *Cassidy*."

Hearing that, Will's stricken expression melted, and she actually managed to smile.

Kadma saw that Will was still tightly clutching the diary. She reached out and did the only thing she could – she covered Will's hand with her own, pressing Halinor's diary, and all its wisdom and good intentions, closer to Will's heart . . . and the Heart of Candracar.

EIGHT

The next day was Friday. With classes over for the week, the grounds around the Sheffield Institute became an instant outdoor party. Students exited the building laughing and shouting. Kids broke out skateboards and played Hacky Sack or pickup soccer. Best friends and couples made plans for the weekend or said goodbye until Monday.

But the upbeat atmosphere didn't reach every part of the school lawn. On a secluded section of grass, under the library window, Irma sat in a circle with three of her best friends – Cornelia, Taranee, and Hay Lin. Will *should* have been there, too, but she was absent from school that day. So Hay Lin alone had to update the rest of them on what had happened in Fadden Hills the day before.

Whoa, Irma thought as Hay Lin spoke of the blackbird butler and the tale of supernatural crime and punishment. She doubted that any of the other kids on the Sheffield lawn were talking about similar things.

Then again, she thought, it fits right in with the wonderful world of being a Guardian. . . . I mean, while my classmates have been hanging at the mall, I've been fighting giant snake-men and hiding in closets watching my maths teacher turn into a kind of cockroach and jump through a portal to another dimension.

As Irma continued to listen to Hay Lin, however, her lighthearted mood began to change. The murder of Cassidy was not exactly funny stuff. And the story about Kadma and Halinor being banished from Candracar made her blood boil!

How could the Oracle have made two Guardians outcasts, she wondered, just for disagreeing with him?

When Hay Lin finished her story, Irma cleared her throat loudly. She made a show of closing her eyes, touching her thumbs to her forefingers, and crossing her legs in a Zen-like pose.

"The fate of the universe is in our hands!" Irma intoned, doing her best impersonation of the great and powerful Oracle. "You are the chosen ones, and yada, yada, yada . . ."

Irma opened her eyes to find the other Guardians staring at her. Not one of them was even smiling. Oh, come on, she thought, laugh at the ethereal dude, will ya? If anyone deserved to be laughed at, it was the Oracle.

"I knew that bigwig, the Oracle, couldn't be trusted!" she told them.

Hay Lin obviously didn't agree. In fact, she looked totally annoyed. "Kadma and Halinor weren't in his good graces, but that doesn't mean anything!" she declared. "My grand-mother always trusted him, and I want to do the same."

Cornelia nodded. "It's true. We've only heard one side of the story. I don't think we should jump to conclusions."

"What?" cried Irma. She couldn't believe that Cornelia, of all people, would come to the Oracle's defense, especially after she'd been so wrecked about his temporarily wiping her memory clear of Caleb. Cornelia had been furious with their cosmic boss over that little magic trick.

Hmmm, thought Irma, tapping her chin. Maybe Cornelia and Hay Lin are just afraid of the Oracle. Maybe they're afraid of becoming outcasts themselves. Well, *I'm* not afraid of him!

"Mr. Know-It-All had to have known that Nerissa could have eliminated Cassidy," Irma argued, "but he gave her the Heart of Candracar anyway. What should we make of that?"

"Maybe he hoped Nerissa wouldn't do it," Cornelia suggested. "He wanted to give her a chance."

"Yeah," said Hay Lin, "everybody makes mistakes. Even people who *never* make them."

Irma's hands curled into fists. They just didn't get it, she thought. "Kicking Kadma and Halinor out of Candracar was really low!" she said.

Hearing those words, Cornelia and Hay Lin frowned and clammed up. Irma got the feeling they really did agree with that part, but just didn't want to say it out loud.

Irma glanced at Taranee, who was leaning back on her elbows, her legs stretched out in front of her on the grass. The fire girl had yet to voice an opinion, so Irma asked her, "What do you think, Taranee?"

Taranee lifted her chin and peered through her large, round glasses with the expression of a disappointed teacher. "I think we should be taking care of Will right now."

Hay Lin hugged her knees. "She said she'd try the old thermometer-on-the-lightbulb trick."

"Faking a fever?" Irma laughed at that one. "It never works for me. My mum's too sharp." She got to her feet. "Call me a buttinsky, but I think I'll stop by to see her. What do you say?"

"I can't. I have a dentist's appointment," Hay Lin replied. All week Hay Lin had been complaining about the prospect of getting braces. Irma knew it and was about to make a joke. But Hay Lin raised a warning finger. "And no wisecracks!"

Irma shrugged. "Cornelia?" she asked, bending down to rest her hands on Corny's shoulders.

Cornelia shook her head. "I have to finish

all of my homework. Otherwise my parents *won't* be going out of town."

Parents going out of town just might be the happiest string of words in the English language, Irma thought. That and *Attention, students: classes are canceled for the day!*

"Really?" said Taranee. "They're leaving you all alone?"

"They're going away for the weekend," Cornelia explained, "but my mum's already told our neighbour, who's going to check in on me. The good thing is, they're taking Lilian."

Irma filed that little nugget away. Cornelia's high-rise apartment was a very cool place. And she was going to be alone in it all weekend? What potential! Parties, sleepovers, anything was possible. *But,* thought Irma, now is not the time to plan the fun. Now is the time to sniff out the reason Will was too upset to come to school.

There was more to that story than Hay Lin was letting on. Irma was sure of it. And she intended to uncover the details. . . . She just didn't want to do it alone.

"Taranee?" Irma grinned. "Weren't *you* the one who wanted to make sure Will was OK?"

Taranee's expression turned defensive. She pushed her glasses up her nose. "Yeah," she admitted. "But maybe she'd rather be alone for a while."

Irma folded her arms. Taranee loved reading and books, and Irma knew exactly what to say to hook her for sure – "So, like, you're *not* dying to find out what's written in Halinor's diary?"

Taranee couldn't help raising her eyebrows.

Gotcha! Irma thought.

"Come on!" she cried with a laugh. "You can't convince me you're not interested. Your face is an open book."

"Um . . ." Taranee tried to look away.

But Irma shook her head. "Lie all you want, but I'm not buying it."

Finally, Taranee gave up and cracked a smile. "OK," she said.

"Great!" said Irma, pulling Taranee to her feet. She could hardly wait to get over to Will's apartment and start asking questions. "Let's go!"

As the Guardians broke up and headed in different directions, Irma rubbed her hands together.

Gee, she joked to herself, I wonder why I'm

such a sucker for a mystery. Could it be because my dad's a police sergeant?

She smiled. No, she thought. It was because she was a Guardian, and she needed to find out some answers.

NINE

Sitting on the couch in Will's living room, Taranee yawned. I have *got* to get some sleep soon, she thought. These nightmares have been messing up my ability to concentrate. If I don't catch some substantial z's, my grade point average is going to sink faster than a concrete balloon.

"Would you like some more juice?" asked Will's mom.

Next to Taranee on the couch, Irma nodded. Yawning again, Taranee nodded, too. Mrs. Vandom filled their glasses from the pitcher on the coffee table.

Taranee pushed up her glasses and realised it was hard to look at Will's mother without thinking of Mr.

Collins. Everyone knew Mrs. Vandom was dating their history teacher. And Taranee could sort of see why. Mrs. Vandom was very pretty, with long, dark hair, and she wasn't too old or anything like that, either.

Irma took a sip of her refilled juice glass. Then she smiled up at Will's mother. "Thanks, Mrs. Vandom," she said. "Will she be long?"

"No," Mrs. Vandom replied. "Will is just finishing her shower, and then she'll be all yours. In the meantime, help yourselves."

Will's mother tossed her long, dark hair and gestured to the plate of fresh-baked chocolate-chip biscuits on the coffee table in front of them. Taranee rubbed her tired eyes. Was she imagining it, or had Will's mother just *sneered* at them?

She shook her head clear. I must have imagined it, she thought. Will's mother has always been super nice. All the nightmares that I've been having are starting to make me paranoid!

"Yum!" Irma cried.

Taranee was not surprised to see Irma shove two biscuits into her mouth at once, then immediately reach for a third. Leave it to Irma to still have an appetite at a moment like this, she thought. If she kept it up, they'd have to rename her Guardian of munchies. Irma probably hadn't eaten much of her school lunch – a common enough occurrence, given the dubious dishes the Sheffield cafeteria attempted to serve them.

"Wese biscuits aw weally goob! Wight, Tawnee?" Irma said with a mouth full of food.

Irma's cheeks looked like a chipmunk's! Taranee had to laugh. Well, she thought, I guess I'd better try one. I don't want to be rude.

Taranee reached for a biscuit and bit into it. It was deliciously warm and sweet and gooey. Wow, she thought, I can really see why Irma's shoveling them in so heartily.

"They're delicious!" she told Mrs. Vandom. After gobbling up the first, she quickly reached for a second and a third.

Glancing up to smile at Will's mom, Taranee noticed something strange in the woman's expression – something a little *angry*, maybe. She had perched herself on the arm of the couch and folded her arms. Her stare was really intense, too, as if she were waiting for something interesting to happen.

"I'm happy you like the biscuits," she told

the girls. "I was afraid I added too much . . .
poison."

Poison? Taranee froze. I did *not* hear that!
Did I?

"What?" cried Irma, spitting out the food in
her mouth. "Ugh!"

Suddenly, Taranee realised that the poison
was gradually closing up her throat. She was
choking. She couldn't breathe! Then she
looked up, and what she saw made her blood
run ice cold. The woman looming over them
was wearing the same clothes as Will's mother
had been. She had the same long, dark hair,
too. But her face had completely changed. Mrs.
Vandom had transformed into –

"Nerissa!" rasped Irma.

"Yes," said Nerissa, "But relax! The sub-
stance you've just ingested won't take effect for
a few minutes."

Taranee's hands went to her throat. She was
terrified, frantic. . . . She couldn't take a breath!
In two minutes, she was sure to pass out and
suffocate.

Nerissa didn't give her a clue. Hovering over
the girls, she radiated pure hatred. She stared
at them with an evil, mocking smile and asked,

"In the meantime, would you like something to drink?"

"Would you like some more juice?"

Taranee opened her eyes to find a woman with long, dark hair looming over her. "Aaaaagh!" she cried.

"No!" Irma shouted. The pitcher of juice hit the floor as the two girls dived off the couch in terror.

"S – sorry!" said Will's mother with wide eyes. "I didn't mean to startle you. I guess you two . . . um . . . dozed off."

"What?" said Taranee, scratching her head.

"Huh?" said Irma. "We fell asleep?"

Mrs. Vandom pointed towards Will's bedroom. "It's just that Will's almost done with her shower, and I – "

"You were trying to find a way to wake us up without embarrassing us," said Irma. "Of course!"

Taranee sighed with relief. The dream had been so very real. "Th – thanks, Mrs. Vandom. We've been having some pretty bad nightmares . . . and um – " Taranee was so shaken she was about to blurt out how the evil former Guardian

Nerissa had tried to kill them by poisoning the chocolate-chip biscuits. Luckily, Irma cut her off!

"We had a really big lunch!" Irma lied. "An afternoon nap is just what we needed!"

"I see," said Will's mother, as she picked up the fallen pitcher. "Go on into Will's room. She'll be right there."

Exchanging a quick glance. Irma and Taranee left the living room and moved down the hall. Taranee could tell they were both thinking the same thing: *Talk about freaky!*

They entered Will's bedroom, and Taranee's thoughts shifted to Will. She was the reason they'd come there in the first place, and Taranee was honestly worried about her good friend. Will wasn't the type of girl to skip school. So whatever was going on with her must have been pretty bad, she thought.

Will walked into the room wearing a blue terry-cloth bathrobe, towel-drying her wet hair.

Before Taranee could ask how Will was feeling, a flood of words came out of Irma's mouth as she described what had just happened. Typical of the water girl, thought Taranee.

"You *both* had the same dream?" asked Will

when Irma was through talking.

"It wasn't just any dream," said Irma. "It was a dream Nerissa made up."

Taranee rubbed her chin in thought. "Maybe it happened because we fell asleep right next to each other."

Will's eyes narrowed at that. "Sounds like an interesting deduction to me. We've got to tell the others about it!"

"Let's talk magic shop later on," Irma suggested with a wink. "How are *you*?"

Wrapping the big white towel into a turban around her damp hair, Will plopped down on her bed. "My mum figured out that my being sick was just an excuse not to go to school."

"Uh-oh," said Irma. "So what's your punishment?"

"Nothing," Will replied. "She must have sensed I was feeling pretty down."

"A perceptive, understanding mother," said Irma with an exaggerated sigh. "Some people have all the luck."

"And what about the, um . . . the diary?" asked Taranee. She could see that Will was OK. Actually, better than OK. And that was sort of surprising – in a good way.

"Want to take a look?" asked Will, pointing to her desk. "It's over there."

Taranee walked over to the leather-bound book on top of Will's desk. She picked it up, adjusted her glasses, and began leafing through the pages.

"You sure you don't mind?" asked Irma, watching Taranee. "Isn't it something private between you and Halinor?"

Will spread her hands and shrugged. "Maybe it is, and maybe it isn't. But I can't tell, because – "

"Hey," Taranee interrupted, staring at the open book. "What is this written in? Martian dialect?"

"That's just what I was about to tell you," said Will. "I can't understand a single word."

Taranee sighed. For a minute there, she'd been hopeful that the diary would hold the answer to fighting Nerissa. For all she knew, maybe it did. But the Guardians certainly couldn't read it.

As she felt another yawn coming on, Taranee shuddered in fear. The last thing she wanted to do at that moment was sleep. Sleeping meant dreaming, and dreaming meant facing Nerissa in her nightmares. She knew Will and Irma felt exactly the same way.

We *can't* go on like this! Taranee thought in frustration. How are we ever going to escape Nerissa now?

"You really don't have *any* idea what this diary says?" Taranee asked Will desperately. "Not even a guess?"

Will shrugged. She crossed the room and pointed to the pages. "From the pictures, I'd guess it's talking about planets . . . and stars."

Looking at the pages, Taranee wasn't convinced. One thing she did know for sure was that the key to understanding Nerissa might be hidden somewhere in the coded pages of the book in her hand. They had to figure out what the message said . . . every last word.

TEN

"No way!" Hay Lin exclaimed. "No stars! You can't be serious!"

"There are lots of other models," Hay Lin's mother told her daughter as they strolled along the wide, concrete sidewalk. "Look at the brochure the dentist gave you."

Hay Lin squeezed her eyes shut. I already looked at that stupid brochure, she wanted to scream. We waited so long for the dentist to see me, I practically memorised it!

Ugh, she thought. I can't imagine it. Braces. Years of metal brackets and rubber bands twisting tighter and tighter. Years of not being able to eat popcorn at the movies, or chew caramels or gum. Years of getting the food I *do* eat all jammed up inside them. Years of Uriah and his crew of antisocial creeps calling me Brace Face, Magnet Teeth, Barbara Wire, and Metal Mouth.

But the worst part, the *absolute* worst part, is imagining how Eric will look at me the first time he sees me wearing them!

A year ago, Hay Lin hadn't really cared what boys thought of her, mainly because she hadn't thought much of boys. They'd all seemed so dorky and ridiculous to her, laughing like donkeys in the halls at school, chewing with their mouths open at lunch, burping in the middle of class to be funny.

Hay Lin was officially the last member of W.I.T.C.H. to get a crush. Until she met Eric Lyndon, she had thought boys were generally gawky and gross and good only for making crude jokes and picking at scabs.

But Eric had changed all that. It had happened the moment she'd bumped into him over summer vacation. *Literally,* bumped into him!

Eric had been on his motorbike. And she'd been on her Rollerblades, weaving her way down the street while trying to balance an ice-cream cone in her hand. When the back of his bike accidentally caught the strap of her purple shoulder bag, she'd been hooked – in more ways than one.

That same evening, Eric had come by the Silver Dragon restaurant to see Hay Lin. She was stunned when he'd said hello to their head chef, Fang, in *Chinese*!

Eric had explained that he'd travelled all over the world with his parents. He'd said he didn't know many Chinese words, but Fang had been impressed. And so had Hay Lin. Then Eric had taken Hay Lin to the Heatherfield Observatory so that they could watch that night's meteor shower.

The shooting stars had been amazing, exploding like fireworks in the sky. And the observatory, high on a hill in Heatherfield Park, had been the perfect place to see them. The observatory was also the place where Eric now lived with his grandfather, the astronomer Zachary Lyndon.

Ever since that night, Hay Lin's heart had beat a little bit faster when she thought of Eric Lyndon. *Yes,* she had to admit it. Eric was her first real crush. She really, really liked him. And she knew he liked her. But how much he liked her, and where it would lead, was still up in the air. And nobody knew better than Hay Lin how quickly winds could change.

What if Eric hates me in braces? Hay Lin asked herself. And even if he doesn't, why would he ever want to kiss a girl with a mouth full of wires? Would he really like me enough to risk electrocution?

No, Hay Lin concluded. I am *not* going to have anything attached to my mouth that might set off a metal detector!

"Mom, read my lips!" she shouted. "There's *no way* I'm going to wear braces!"

Her mother didn't even glance up from the *Braces and You!* brochure. "If you don't want the ones with the stars," she said, pointing to the glossy photos that illustrated the different styles, "we could ask him to make you one with your name written across it."

Really, thought Hay Lin. How is it that I shout at the top of my lungs and my mother *still* does not hear me?

It was not the first time Hay Lin had found herself missing her grandmother. Since she was a baby, her parents had been constantly busy running their restaurant. From morning till night there was always something they had to take care of: some sauce to prepare, special party to serve, or mess to clean up. Then there was shopping and billing and payroll. Always something!

It was her grandmother who gave real time to Hay Lin – to listen, give advice, or tell her some magical story to make her problems seem far away.

If she were here now, she would *hear me*, thought Hay Lin. She would *listen*. But, most of all, she would never, *ever* suggest something as totally *geeky* and *babyish* as having my name written across my mouth!

Hay Lin rolled her eyes at her mother's idea. "Sure!" she replied. "That way all I'll have to do to introduce myself to somebody is smile!"

By now Hay Lin and her mother had reached the street corner. Hay Lin's mother walked up to the front door of their restaurant and pulled it open. Hay Lin stormed through, her jaw set in an angry pout.

In two hours the Silver Dragon's dining room would be packed with regulars. The air would be filled with the scents of garlic and sizzling pork, peanut oil, and fragrant tea. The buzz of customer conversations would mix with the clinking of china plates and the clicking of wooden chopsticks.

At this moment, however, the dining room was empty. Hay Lin marched by the empty tables, which were covered only with cleaned and pressed tablecloths. Her mother would soon begin placing the dishes, glasses, and chopsticks at every setting. Chen, one of the kitchen workers, was already pitching in to help prepare the dining room. He was just in the process of placing a vase of fresh flowers on every table.

"In any case," said Hay Lin's mother, following on her daughter's heels, "you've got to pick a style. Your health comes first."

Hay Lin clenched her fists. "What a totally *lame* thing to say," she replied. "Typical of someone who would never have worn braces when she was young!"

Hay Lin's mother frowned – and finally acknowledged *hearing* her daughter. "I won't allow you to talk to me like this. When I was your age, I couldn't afford luxuries like that!"

Luxuries? Hay Lin repeated to herself. "Oh, no!" she muttered aloud. "Here we go again!"

She could tell her mother was about to pull out one of those old, dusty stories of having to struggle and do without. Hay Lin gritted her teeth.

I just can't win, she thought. My mother tells me I'm *lucky* to make me feel *guilty*. Then I'm supposed to suddenly see everything her way and do what she says!

Chen began to laugh, and Hay Lin turned to face him. The man was big and stout, with dark eyebrows as bushy as his mustache, and a head as smooth as a billiard ball. He ambled over, his large, blue apron tied around his substantial girth. "In my days, those kinds of contraptions weren't necessary," he declared.

Hay Lin's pout turned into a grin. "You tell her, Chen!"

"And I'm still smiling at life!" The big man pointed to the wide smile on his face.

Staring into his mouth, Hay Lin gulped. Chen's smile was enthusiastic – but it was far from pretty. Many of his teeth were missing, and the ones that weren't were crooked or chipped.

"Yeah, Chen," Hay Lin said weakly. "Thanks for the support. . . ." She forced herself to keep grinning until her mother left the room.

OK, Hay Lin thought with a sigh, I don't want a mouth like Chen's. And I'm sure Eric wouldn't want me to have a mouth like Chen's, either! But do I really have to wear braces? . . . And are *these* my only *choices*?

"Oh!" said Chen, reaching into his back pocket. "Before I forget. There's a letter for you."

"Huh? For me?" Hay Lin took the envelope and studied it. When she saw the familiar star logo on the return address, she caught her breath. "From the Rising Star Foundation?" she said.

Instantly, Hay Lin forgot about her anxieties over getting braces. If she had learned one thing about being a Guardian, it was to put things in her own life aside when Guardian business called.

And this *has* to be Guardian business, Hay Lin told herself. Because there's only one person I know who lives at this address.

"But what could Kadma want from me?" she whispered.

ELEVEN

Welcome to yet another emergency meeting of the Guardians, thought Cornelia.

The five Guardians were currently gathered around their regular booth at the Golden diner – home of the best triple-decker burgers in Heatherfield and the site of Will's first official date with Matt. It also happened to be the Guardians' emergency meeting place of choice.

Gee, wondered Cornelia, tapping her cheek, I wonder how many of these super-urgent get-togethers we've had now. There've been so many, they're actually starting to feel routine!

The girls ordered some drinks and snacks, and updated each other on what had happened since they'd parted earlier that day. Irma and Taranee told everyone about having the same dream on Will's couch. And Hay Lin produced the letter she'd received from Kadma.

"It's just a little note," Hay Lin told the girls, "but it seems important."

Cornelia wasn't going to argue. Nerissa's bad dreams were turning their waking lives into nightmares. Anything that might lead the Guardians to a way to defeat her was worth considering.

"Read the letter out loud, Hay Lin," Cornelia suggested.

Hay Lin nodded and pulled the letter from its envelope. *"Nerissa lives in the world of nightmares,"* she read. *"But that is also her weakness."*

Cornelia pricked up her ears at the word *weakness.* She'd always thought the key to defeating Nerissa would be finding her Achilles' heel, her weakness. Now here was Kadma giving W.I.T.C.H. a clue to finding it. But what exactly was that clue?

Nerissa lives in the world of nightmares, Cornelia silently repeated to herself while the others sat quietly. For at least a minute, no one said a word. Taranee and Will sipped their sodas.

Irma munched a french fry. Finally, she asked, "Anyone get it?"

"Hmmm," Cornelia said at last. "Maybe I do." All eyes were on her as she leaned forward and laid out her theory. "This afternoon, the reason Taranee and Irma had the *same* dream was that they fell asleep next to each other. . . . We know Nerissa can truly attack us, especially when she's in that dimension."

"Right," agreed Will. "The first time I met her, I was dreaming and she left her mark on me."

Cornelia nodded. "I think Kadma's trying to tell us that the opposite can happen, too."

Will's face brightened. "Of course! If it's possible to affect the real world from inside a dream – "

" – The exact opposite could probably happen," Irma quickly added. "I get it!"

"So," said Taranee, peering uneasily at Cornelia through her glasses. "You want us to attack Nerissa in the world of nightmares?"

Cornelia nodded. "It's better than going to dig her out of Mount Thanos. Plus, if we face her together, maybe she won't have a way to escape."

Just then, Cornelia glanced up from their booth and noticed a popular boy from school standing next to their table. He was wearing a blue sweatshirt and holding a tray of food. On his face was an expression of total bafflement. Cornelia guessed he'd been walking by and heard them talking about other "dimensions" and about attacking someone in a "world of nightmares."

Cornelia gave him a weak smile. "A new game," she told the handsome football player. "Fantasy role-playing. Ever heard of it?"

The boy rolled his eyes in disgust and walked away.

Cornelia exhaled a tense breath. I cannot believe I just did that, she thought. I told one of the popular kids that I'm a fantasy-game geek! And I actually hoped he bought it!

Cornelia glanced around the booth at each of her friends. They were all so different. Will, a quiet tomboy. Irma, an outspoken clown. Hay Lin, kooky and flighty. And Taranee, studious and serious. And then there's me, thought Cornelia – Miss Popular, Miss Practical.

Sometimes Cornelia wished her life could be more normal.

Just a bit! I mean, *really*, she thought. Look at all these people gulping onion rings and slurping milk shakes. Their biggest concerns are what to shop for next at the mall and how to get rid of their latest zit. And what is my life like? Oh, let's see . . . I'm trying to figure out exactly how to defeat a supernaturally evil crone. I'm in love with a guy who was once a flower and lives in another world. And on a good day . . . I have wings.

Cornelia was about to start really feeling sorry for herself when Irma blurted out, "What a genius!"

Whoa, thought Cornelia, why is everybody grinning at me?

"So there really is a brain underneath all those golden locks," Irma continued. "All we need to do is fall asleep all together!"

"What do you say we have a nice pajama party at my house tonight?" Cornelia suggested. She was glad that everyone seemed to be on board with her plan.

"Right!" Irma cried, bouncing up and down on the seat cushion. "Your folks won't be there, and we can take care of your snoopy old neighbour, no sweat!"

Cornelia laughed. From the moment she'd mentioned the fact that her parents were going away for the weekend, Irma had been salivating for something like this. "Um, somebody better strap Irma down," Cornelia warned. "Or she's liable to bounce up through the ceiling."

"Ha-ha, Corny, very funny," said Irma and threw a fry across the table.

Cornelia laughed as she easily dodged it.

To be left alone for the entire weekend was a huge responsibility, and Cornelia knew it. She didn't plan on going behind her parents' backs with a pyjama party or anything like that. She intended to tell them she was having friends over. Her neighbour would certainly tell her parents if she didn't, anyway! . . . She'd just have to leave out the part about battling an immortal evil.

I'll bring over some DVDs," Irma told the girls. "And we can pop popcorn. And there's this new pizza place that delivers to Cornelia's neighbourhood. I read about it online last week. They do this veggie pizza with eggplant and smoked mozzarella – "

"Eggplant!" Taranee cried, making a sour face. "Not for me. And smoked cheese doesn't sound very appetising, either."

"I have to agree with Taranee on that one," said Will.

"Fine!" said Irma, throwing up her hands. "You can have your boring pepperoni and extra cheese then!"

"Pepperoni may be boring," Taranee countered. "But it is the most popular pizza topping – statistically speaking."

"There you go," said Will with a laugh. "You can't argue with statistics."

Irma smirked. "Just because something is statistically *popular* doesn't mean it's *good*."

"Guys, don't worry," said Cornelia, breaking up the pizza topping debate. "My mother stocked plenty of munchies in the pantry before she left."

"Great," said Will.

Everyone looked pretty pleased with the pyjama-party plans. Only Hay Lin seemed distracted. "Something's funny about this," she said, still staring at Kadma's letter.

"What?" asked Will.

Hay Lin flipped one of her silky black pigtails over her shoulder. "Why would Kadma entrust a message like this to snail mail?"

Will rolled her eyes. "You met her, Hay Lin. She's living a pretty isolated life. I doubt she even knows how to use e-mail."

"She could have called," Hay Lin pointed out.

Will stole a french fry from Irma's plate. "You didn't notice she's got a personality that's – how can I put this? A bit *difficult*?"

"Why are you tiptoeing around it?" Irma said. "Go ahead and say it. She's a chronic grouch. And she's obviously not crazy about us."

"I don't think that's it," said Hay Lin.

"Well," said Cornelia. She leaned forward. "I say we give this plan a shot. Maybe we'll just end up sleeping, but at least we won't be alone."

Everyone nodded in unison.

Awesome! Cornelia thought. Even though we five are very different . . . and we don't always get along, when it truly counts we really do make an *excellent* team!

TWELVE

As the Guardians left the Golden, Will felt a tug on her sleeve. She turned to find Hay Lin smiling at her.

"I think I know who might be able to read Halinor's diary," she told Will.

"Who?" Will asked. She'd brought the diary with her to show Cornelia. But she'd been as stumped as the rest of the Guardians. Will was pretty much up for trying anything now.

"We have about an hour before the place closes to the public," said Hay Lin, glancing at her watch.

"What place?" Will asked.

But Hay Lin just turned and waved. "Follow me!"

She hopped on to her bike. Will

hopped on hers, and the two girls rode off, pedaling hard into Heatherfield Park and all the way up a steep rise. At the very top, a grand old building overlooked the park below, like a castle dominating the countryside.

So *that's* where we're heading, Will realised. The Heatherfield Observatory!

"Hay Lin, *who* are we going to see in there?" Will cried.

"You'll see," Hay Lin called back, and the girls continued pedaling.

Will had never been to the observatory before. The white granite building looked supremely majestic in the red-orange light of the setting sun. Formal columns lined its stone front, and its great domed roof could be seen for miles around.

When Will and Hay Lin arrived, they parked their bikes at the base of the steps and climbed up to the arched entryway. The front doors were unlocked, and the girls wandered into the lobby. They crossed the marble floor and approached the front desk.

"Can I help you?" asked a barrel-chested security guard.

Hay Lin said, "We're here to see Eric

Lyndon. May we go in, please?"

The guard eyed the two of them. "Both of you?"

"Yes," said Hay Lin. "I'm actually his – " She stopped abruptly and glanced nervously at Will. "We're his *friends*."

The guard smiled. "I see."

He sent the girls through the large, main hall and up a grand staircase. The girls climbed and climbed and climbed. The marble stairs turned into a narrow set of spiral steps. Hay Lin and Will kept climbing.

When they reached the highest level, they found a single door. It was slightly ajar, and Will could see part of the room inside. Star maps hung on the walls, but most of the space appeared to be dominated by a huge telescope.

"Knock, knock!" Hay Lin called.

Eric Lyndon, Hay Lin's new crush, opened the door.

Will could hear the nervousness in Hay Lin's voice as she said hello.

Hay Lin quickly explained why they had dropped by, and Will pulled out Halinor's leather-bound diary.

"Fascinating!" Eric exclaimed as he leafed

through page after page of planets, stars, and strange, undecipherable symbols.

Will was a little nervous about this, but Hay Lin seemed sure he could help. "Then you understand something of this, Eric?" Hay Lin asked hopefully.

"Nothing at all!" he replied. "But I can give you a hand. I'm not able to decipher runes . . . but this material will definitely interest my grandpa."

Hay Lin bit her lip. "The p – professor?" she stammered.

"That's what they call him," said Eric. "But his name's Zachary Lyndon. Did I already introduce you to him?"

"Um . . . no . . ." said Hay Lin, shifting her feet and scratching her head. "But I've heard a lot about him."

Will bit her lip to keep from smiling. Hay Lin wasn't acting all nervous and goofy because of the diary. It was pretty obvious she was crushin' on Eric big-time. Will remembered acting just as silly when she had first started talking to Matt.

Watching Eric, Will could see why Hay Lin liked him so much. He was tall, intelligent, and seemingly very kind. He had big brown eyes, dark, tousled hair, and a really nice smile. He was *almost* as appealing as Matt.

Will smiled thinking of her crush. She hadn't spent any real time with him since this whole Nerissa thing had started. She really missed him, too. And, for some reason, seeing Hay Lin smiling nervously up at Eric made her miss him even more.

Eric turned to Will. "I'll be happy to talk to my grandpa," he told her. "But it's your book. It's really up to you to agree."

"I agree!" Will quickly replied. "Totally! Although I wouldn't want to be a bother . . ."

Eric's smile was reassuring. "He'll be happy to help. Grandpa loves solving puzzles."

He headed for the door, still flipping through the pages of the diary. Will and Hay Lin followed.

"Thanks for asking Eric to help, Hay Lin," whispered Will as they walked back down the spiral staircase they had just come up.

"I'm always happy to see him again," Hay Lin admitted. She spoke in an even softer whisper. "I just hope he can solve your problem."

"So, what can you tell me about Eric's

grandfather?" Will whispered, making sure to speak quietly so Eric wouldn't hear them. "You acted so weird when you heard his name."

"He's a scientist. An astronomer, to be exact. I hate meeting relatives. . . ." She shrugged. "In any case, there are totally strange stories about him. Really spooky ones."

Will was dying to hear more, but they had to catch up with Eric. His long legs were moving faster now that they'd reached the bottom of the spiral staircase. He led the way down a long hallway lined with cream-coloured marble columns.

"I'm sure there's something that can help all of us in those formulas," Will told Hay Lin. At least, I *hope* so, she added to herself.

Hay Lin nodded and checked her watch again. "Then we'd better hurry. They might come in handy at our pyjama party!"

The girls caught up to Eric as he stopped in front of an old wooden door; he turned the doorknob and announced, "Come right in, and be careful on the steps! Grandpa's down in the basement."

Will stepped inside and gaped in confusion at the narrow, dimly lit stairwell. This wasn't like any other part of the grand, airy observatory. No polished marble. No white granite. No stately columns. Just dingy bricks and a bare lightbulb. She exchanged a dubious glance with Hay Lin, who peered down the staircase with the same confused expression as Will.

What had Hay Lin just said about Eric's grandfather? Will thought. Something about strange, spooky stories?

Will suddenly wasn't at all sure they'd done the right thing. As Eric led the way again, she followed, but not happily.

What are we doing? Where are we going? How is any of this going to help? she asked herself as she made her way down the musty, narrow staircase.

Oh, my gosh, I know what this reminds me of, she thought: all those scary movies, where the girls get led by the seemingly innocent guy into a room full of flesh-eating zombies. *Aaaaaaagh!*

Eric laughed when he turned around and saw Will's and Hay Lin's freaked-out faces. "Don't worry!" he reassured them. "I'm not taking you into the dark dungeons of the observatory. I promise!"

When they reached the bottom, Eric put his hand on the release bar of a steel fire door. "My grandpa thought that down here was the perfect place to set up a new planetarium," he told the girls with an excited smile. "We're just finishing the last of the special effects. Let me know what you think."

Ker-chunk!

Eric pushed open the heavy door, and Will and Hay Lin stepped into another world – or, at least, what *felt* like another world.

Projectors and green screens made the entire basement of the vast observatory into a three-dimensional representation of the earth's solar system. These images seemed real – as if they were suspended all around them.

"Wow!" cried Will. "This is way cool!"

Mercury, Venus, Earth, Mars, the asteroid belt, and a billion stars beyond . . . they were spinning in orbits so close she could practically reach out and touch them!

"It's like . . . like floating around in space!" cried Hay Lin.

Will couldn't believe what was right in front of her. The vast blue-blackness seemed to go on forever. It was like Candracar, she thought, and its endless blue sky. She couldn't help remembering the astonishment she'd felt on her first trip there – and when she'd first met the Oracle.

"It's all a simulation," a deep voice suddenly boomed from somewhere in the blue-black vastness. "Ordinary people aren't very interested in astronomy. In fact, I'm surprised girls your age are curious about the subject."

Will gathered her courage and moved farther into "space." It wasn't easy. Her balance was off, because she couldn't see the floor, only feel it. And her eyesight needed to adjust to the bright glow of the "planets." Once she got her bearings, however, she was able to make out an old man with white hair, a bushy white mustache, and steel-framed glasses.

"This light show should raise at least a bit of interest among youngsters, don't you think?" the professor asked Will.

Will quickly nodded. Hay Lin caught up and she nodded, too.

In the end, Professor Lyndon was very nice, despite Will's initial fears about how he would react to the diary. He agreed to look at the leather-bound diary, just not right away. So Will and Hay Lin had no choice. They politely said goodbye, then headed off to their pajama party.

The mysteries of Halinor's diary were now in the hands of a man who enjoyed creating his very own universe – and who might have the key to unlocking the diary's secrets.

THIRTEEN

Cornelia pressed the saltshaker into the woman's hand. "You're welcome, Miss Prottinger!"

Yikes, thought Cornelia. Will my neighbour *ever* get the hint that maybe I want a little *privacy*?

"Wait a moment," the woman cried. "I – "

Nope, Cornelia realised, she'll never get it. What a total busybody! *"Goodnight,* Miss Prottinger," she said, louder this time.

Gee, thought Cornelia, what else could I do to give the woman a hint? I know. She placed her shoulder against the front door and *pushed* with all her might. The door closed with a solid click. And Cornelia quickly threw the lock in place.

Lounging on the couch across the room, Hay Lin was impressed. "How did you know she was going to ask you for salt?" she asked.

"Process of elimination," Cornelia replied with a shrug. "Today she peeked in with excuses of butter, flour, and sugar! The only ingredient missing was salt, so she's got to be finished now."

Irma spoke from the blue chair in the living room. "Do you think she's doing this to make your folks happy, or for personal pleasure?"

"No doubt it's because Miss Pottinger is a certified snoop," Cornelia told them as she glided back into the spacious living room of her parents' high-rise apartment. Her nightgown was long and flowing, and bright blue to match her eyes. All of her friends were wearing their nicest pyjamas for the sleepover, as well.

Irma wore sky-blue baby-dolls with ruffles across the bottom and matching floppy slippers. Taranee wore burnt-orange loose pants and a long-sleeved top that beautifully set off her cocoa skin. Hay Lin seemed a little cold in her spaghetti-strap two-piece. And Will looked ever the gawky tomboy in her frog-green boxers and tank.

That outfit is just *so* Will, thought Cornelia with a private little smile. Suddenly feeling like a mother hen, she announced, "And now, it's bedtime, guys!"

"Yeah, sure," said Taranee. She punched a goose-down pillow, propped it against the arm of the couch, and sank down into it. "That's going to be *real* easy. I'm wide awake."

Cornelia folded her arms. So far that night, the girls had watched a movie on DVD, downed a big bowl of popcorn, and devoured two pepperoni pizzas. At that point in a *typical* pyjama party, they would have been settling down to a marathon gossip session.

But this wasn't a typical pyjama party, and staying up half the night was out of the question. As far as Cornelia was concerned, the Guardians had had their fun. Now it was time to get down to work – and to the reason they were having a sleepover in the first place.

OK, she thought, so "work" involved more than just falling asleep. Once the girls were in Nerissa's dreamworld, they'd be fighting for their lives against the evil woman.

Cornelia was thinking that under those circumstances, few people would have been eager to go to bed. And apparently, she wasn't the only one who thought so.

"How can you go to sleep knowing what's in store for us?" Taranee asked.

"Yeah," said Irma. "A real nightmare come true, with Nerissa to boot!"

Like the other Guardians, Cornelia was finding it harder and harder to live in two worlds. Outside, the lights of Heatherfield twinkled cheerfully in the summer night. People were out at restaurants, nightclubs, the movies. They were living their lives, enjoying time with their friends or families. The earth world was the only world those people knew. She doubted that any of them ever considered other worlds, other dimensions.

Lucky them, thought Cornelia. They've never heard of the Oracle, Prince Phobos, the rebellion in Meridian, or the Heart of Candracar. They don't wake up every morning with the heavy responsibilities of being a Guardian.

Will stood up and stretched. Her belly showed underneath her frog-green tank. Cornelia was surprised – and impressed – at how relaxed she appeared.

"The only way to handle this," Irma advised, "is not to think too much about it and to try to kill time somehow."

"I agree," said Will. Then she wandered off to explore the large apartment.

Cornelia had to admit, she was proud of her home. Her mother had excellent taste, and there were beautiful antiques all over the pent-house, not to mention a marble column or two, framed mirrors, expensive throw rugs, elabo-rate draperies, and a spectacular view of the city through tall, wraparound windows.

Cornelia faced the others. She noticed that Hay Lin was strangely quiet. Taranee noticed it, too.

"What's wrong, Hay Lin? Are you worried?" Taranee asked.

Hay Lin hugged herself, shivering as if she'd had a chill. "I was thinking about 'Nerissa's Trill,'" Hay Lin replied in a hushed voice. "I'm afraid of hearing it again."

"That's natural," Taranee assured her, "now that you know what it really means."

"It's not just that!" Hay Lin said. "Music normally conjures up memories in my mind, or gives me certain sensations. But the trill . . ."

Her voice trailed off. She rubbed her arms, as if she couldn't shake the cold. "It's as though it was totally devoid of spirit."

"Hey!" Will called from the hallway. "Come take a look at what I found in Cornelia's bedroom!"

Oh, no! Cornelia groaned to herself. How embarrassing.

She knew *exactly* what Will had found, and she felt herself blushing as she followed her friends down the hall.

Taranee made it through the door first. She spied Will sitting on the polished hardwood floor, next to a miniature two-story building filled with tiny pieces of furniture. "Wow! A dollhouse," she cried.

"So *that's* how Cornelia spends her free time," teased Irma.

"Very funny," Cornelia replied. "I'd kept it in the closet until Lilian took it out."

Irma shot her a skeptical look.

Cornelia put her hands on her hips. "I'm telling you, my little sister is the one who's been playing with it."

"Sure, Cornelia," Irma replied with a wink to the others. "Whatever."

Cornelia rolled her eyes in frustration. Sometimes Irma could really make her crazy!

Will reached inside the large dollhouse and began to play with some of the furniture. "Think what you want," she told Irma with a grin, "but now I know how *I'm* going to spend my time waiting to get sleepy."

Taranee, Irma, and Hay Lin acted as though they were way too mature to join Will. Ignoring the dollhouse, they read magazines and played chess on the bed. It was Cornelia herself who finally surrendered to her inner child. She knelt down on the floor next to Will. Together they rearranged the furniture in every room of the dollhouse. And they had *fun* doing it!

Cornelia couldn't help remembering back to a time when the little house and the dolls inside it were the most important things in the world to her. It seemed very long ago now: before the Guardians, before Caleb, even before she'd met Will and Taranee.

When she was little, Cornelia had constantly wished for a time when she would be older, able to lead an exciting life, enjoy adventures, have a boyfriend. She'd longed for a time when her parents and nosy neighbours had no say over her life, when she could make her own important choices, control her own destiny.

Now that she *was* older, however, Cornelia sometimes felt she had even *less* control over her own life, not more, than before. And as far as "important choices" were concerned, now she was *forced* into making them – and she wasn't altogether happy about it.

Basically, things had got a lot more complicated now that she was older. Real life wasn't easy. It wasn't like a dollhouse, where you could place things where you wanted them – and they'd *stay* that way until the next time you wanted to play! . . . No, life was messy.

Cornelia thought of Caleb and all the things that had gone wrong. She thought of the responsibilities of being a Guardian and how she sometimes didn't want them. And the nightmares, for sure, she could do without!

With those gloomy thoughts weighing heavily on her, she found her eyelids drifting closed. Will was already sprawled out on the floor. She'd slipped into sleep admiring the living room that she'd just decorated inside the tiny dollhouse. Hay Lin, Irma, and Taranee had all dozed off on the bed, the game of chess lying unfinished in front of them.

Now Cornelia, too, felt the need for sleep tugging at her. She decided to stretch out on the floor. Propping her head on her arm, she closed her eyes.

Within a few minutes, Cornelia finally joined her friends. She floated through the gates of the real world and entered the realm of dreams.

FOURTEEN

Will opened her eyes to a world that was different . . . yet oddly familiar. She was still sprawled on the floor. But this floor wasn't the polished hardwood floor of Cornelia's bedroom, where she'd fallen asleep. The dream floor was covered in soft, thick, eggshell-coloured carpet, just like the one inside Cornelia's dollhouse.

Will sat up, fluttering her wings in surprise. Power rippled through her longer, stronger limbs. Her frog-green pj's had been replaced by the cool, sophisticated Guardian outfit she loved so much – her short, aqua-green skirt, purple belly-baring blouse with the long, flowing sleeves, and kickin' blue-and-green-striped tights.

Weird, thought Will. She had no

memory of evoking the powers of the Heart of Candracar or of *transforming*. Had the Heart read her intentions as she'd fallen off to sleep?

Will stood up inside the dollhouse and discovered she wasn't the only one dreaming she was a miniaturised Guardian doll. One other Guardian appeared to have made the jump with her. Cornelia stood on the other side of the room, her delicate blue-green wings ruffling nervously. A look of puzzlement crossed her face.

Will glanced around. There were no other Guardians in sight. Just a plastic doll, seated on the gold couch where she'd placed it before drifting off. All the toy furniture she'd been playing with was there, too – the gold stuffed chair and matching ottoman, the glass-topped coffee table, the silver tray with a little tea set on top, complete with tiny cups, saucers, and spoons. Of course, none of it looked tiny now.

"I think the idea of us sleeping in the same place worked," said Will.

Cornelia nodded. "Yeah. If I'm not mistaken, we're *inside* my dollhouse!"

"It looks like it," Will replied. "Although I can't say that's totally reassuring." Because,

Will added to herself, we're shrunk to the size of dolls, and possibly trapped like rats inside one of Nerissa's nightmares!

Cornelia was also searching the room, on the lookout for danger. "Luckily, we've already transformed," she noted.

Will was still concerned about that. Why should we be transformed, she thought, unless it's time for action? Now Will was almost certain that she and Cornelia had been caught in a trap. She searched again for the other Guardians, but nobody else was there, except for the doll sitting on the couch, its plastic face turned so far away that all she could see was the doll's dark, straight hair hanging down.

The doll looked downright creepy to Will. Its hair was a black curtain obscuring its painted features, its plastic arms were in the air, its legs stretched out in front of it.

That doll's as big as I am now, Will thought. Then she shook her head. That's not right, she corrected herself. It's me who's been shrunk down to the size of the doll!

Will felt a sudden jolt of panic. Despite her formidable powers, she felt small and helpless and fragile. She tried to remind herself that she was in a dream, that none of this was real.

Yet she knew that Nerissa had physically hurt her once in a dream, and could do it again. She was also keenly aware of what the evil woman had done to Cassidy and to Caleb. And of what she could do to any of the Guardians with her power.

Despite Will's determination not to be afraid, her pulse fluttered along with her wings. Then the back of her neck tingled, and Will got the feeling she was being watched. Cornelia's tense expression told Will that she, too, sensed that danger was close.

"Better," said a strong, feminine voice in a tone of mocking cruelty. "That's *much* better."

Will and Cornelia whirled to face the couch. They both stared at the only other figure in the room – the plastic doll. As they watched, the figure's head turned, and her curtain of hair parted. A familiar face grinned out at them in place of the painted plastic smile.

Cornelia and Will screamed. "Nerissa!"

"I'm delighted to see you're already transformed," said the former Keeper of the Heart. "That way we're all ready to *play* together."

Will shuddered. Nerissa's real face was

plastered over the plastic doll's body. With her arms stuck up in the air and her legs out, she looked like an evil puppet without strings. Too creepy, Will thought.

"Oh, how thoughtless of me," Nerissa added, from the couch. "You're guests in my nightmare. Can I offer you some tea?"

Nerissa's plastic arms shot out. An explosion of magic energy upset the glass-topped table and sent the silver tea set flying towards the two Guardians.

Cornelia blocked her face with her hands as cups, plates, and spoons were turned into projectiles. Will ducked. A saucer flew past her head like a malignant Frisbee.

"No, thanks," Will replied, forcing the tea set back with a blast of raw Guardian power.

Nerissa's eyes narrowed. Her pleasant demeanor vanished. Now the former Guardian glared at them with a murderous fire. An ancient hatred burned deep inside her, and Will gulped down her panic as she glimpsed its enormity.

"Good," Nerissa purred. "I see that for you girls to feel safe, you have to make sure there are at least *two* of you."

"But there should be more," Will murmured to herself. All five Guardians had fallen asleep in the same room. "There should be more than just us two," she whispered.

Despite her fear, Will crouched in a fighting stance, ready to strike, when a welcome voice cried out –

"Learn to *count!*"

It's Irma! Will realised. The water girl appeared in the room already transformed. Hay Lin and Taranee were on Irma's heels.

Nerissa's eyes registered alarm. "No!" she cried. "You can't *all* be here!"

"Is this dream getting to be too much for you to handle, Nerissa? Deal with it!" said Irma with a snap of her fingers.

With her friends and fellow Guardians around her, Will felt a surge of confidence. The Power of Five was assembled and ready to show Nerissa up! She grinned at the evil crone. "Buy one, get four free, Nerissa," Will mocked. "Take it or leave it!"

Pure hate sizzled in Nerissa's cold, dead eyes. "Then it looks like I'll have to *leave* it," she said.

Nerissa threw out her arms, and the room

appeared to explode. There was a thunderous crack, like a lightning strike, and a white light filled the entire house.

"Aaagh! I can't see," Hay Lin howled.

Will squeezed her eyes shut, but it didn't help. The brightness was unbearable. It was a painful, unnatural glare that penetrated even her closed eyelids. She could tell from the frantic cries of her friends that they were experiencing the same thing.

"It'll pass in a moment," Irma cried. "Let's move."

Suddenly, the Guardians heard a door slam. The brightness instantly disappeared. The couch was empty. Nerissa was gone.

The only door to the room was closed, but it now appeared to be throbbing like a beating heart. Will stepped up to the door. But she hesitated before touching the knob. She turned and faced her friends.

"Cornelia, this is your house," she said. "Where does that door lead?"

Cornelia brushed away a lock of blonde hair. "Well, if this is the living room, that means Nerissa is in – "

Before she could finish, the door opened by

itself. The five girls stared in awe.

"I don't understand," said Cornelia, looking into the next room. "That's supposed to be the kitchen!"

But beyond the threshold, there was no sign of the warm and cosy dollhouse kitchen, with its breakfast nook and modern appliances. Instead, as the Guardians slowly entered the room, they found themselves gazing at an expansive chessboard, its white and black squares stretching out as far as the eye could see.

"Not bad," Irma joked. "If this is the kitchen, then your place is nice and *roomy!*"

Taranee pushed her glasses up on her nose. "This is no kitchen," she said, her six black braids dancing as she shook her head. "This looks more like the chessboard we were using before falling asleep – "

Taranee was interrupted by a crackling burst of magic. The rippling lightning made the squares glow with a strange energy.

What Will saw next sent adrenaline racing through her bloodstream. Dread and determination mixed inside her, quickening her courage and igniting her spirit.

"Down there!" she cried, pointing into the distance.

Nerissa was there waiting for them. The Guardians had to remain strong. The fate of Candracar was in their hands. This was the battle that mattered the most – and they were ready. The Power of Five was ready to fight!

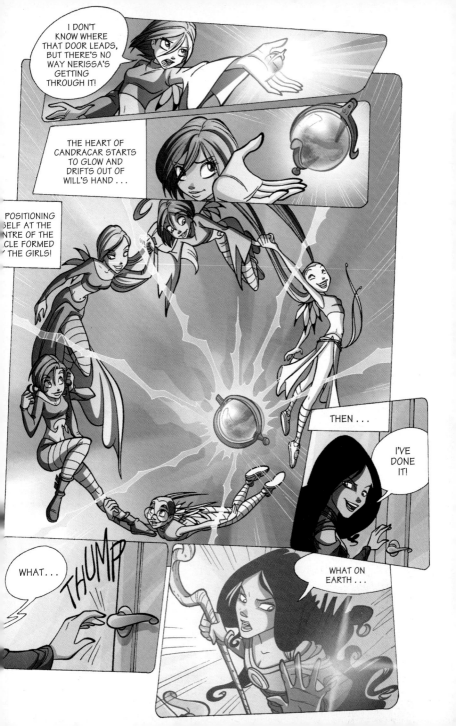

IT DOESN'T LOOK LIKE WE'LL EVER SEE HER AGAIN.

I GUESS WE'LL FIND OUT TONIGHT, WHEN WE TRY TO SLEEP SOUNDLY.

COME ON IN TO THE KITCHEN! THE OTHERS ARE HAVING A GIGANTIC BREAKFAST TO CELEBRATE!

AREN'T YOU HUNGRY, HAY LIN?

NO! THE OTHERS WON'T LISTEN TO ME. IT WAS ALL TOO QUICK. TOO EASY.

COME ON! YOU SAW IT, TOO! THAT WOMAN ANNIHILATED HERSELF RIGHT IN FRONT OF US!

TRUE, THAT'S WHAT WE SAW . . . IN THE DREAM . . .

BUT WHEN I WOKE UP, I HEARD IT AGAIN, WILL . . .

I HEARD "NERISSA'S TRILL"!

TO BE CONTINUED . . .